Married to

Hitler

A Novel

Michael Aaron Rockland

P
H
G
HANSEN PUBLISHING GROUP, LLC

Married to Hitler
Copyright © 2020 by Michael Aaron Rockland

25 24 23 22 21 20   10 9 8 7 6 5 4 3 2 1

ISBN: (HARDCOVER) 978-1-60182-308-3
ISBN: (PAPER) 978-1-60182-309-0
ISBN: (EBOOK) 978-1-60182-310-6

Cover design and book design by Jon Hansen

Hansen Publishing Group, LLC
302 Ryders Lane
East Brunswick, NJ 08816
https://hansenpublishing.com

Works by Michael Aaron Rockland

Creative Nonfiction and Scholarship

The George Washington Bridge: Poetry in Steel (2008, 2019)

The Jews of New Jersey: A Pictorial History (2001) (co-authored with Patricia M. Ard)

Popular Culture: Or Why Study Trash? (1999)

What's American About American Things? (1996)

Looking for America on the New Jersey Turnpike (1989) (co-authored with Angus Kress Gillespie)

Homes on Wheels (1980)

The American Jewish Experience in Literature (1975)

America in the Fifties and Sixties: Julian Marias on the United States (editor) (1972)

Sarmiento's Travels in the United States in 1847 (1970)

Memoir

Navy Crazy (2014)

An American Diplomat in Franco Spain (Spanish edition 2010, American edition 2012)

Snowshoeing Through Sewers (1994)

Fiction

Married to Hitler (2020)

Stones (2009)

A Bliss Case (1989)

Screenplay

Three Days on Big City Waters (1974) (co-authored with Charles Woolfolk)

*In honor of the six million and the few brave souls
who tried to save them.*

Growing up in the shadow of the Holocaust meant that Jewish men…developed a sense of Jewish identity that was strongly associated with human suffering, slaughter and survival.

—Keren McGinity, *Marrying Out*

MARRIED TO HITLER

CHAPTER 1

With his summer classes over at New Jersey University, Adam Levin drove west in his battered, tan '68 Chevy. The car behaved well enough mechanically. Its appearance, combined with the fact he was wearing the same torn jeans and nondescript T-shirt for several days, seemed emblematic of the sorry state of his personal life.

Sure, he wanted to see the country, but this trip was also to put as much distance as possible between himself and his marriage. He supposed his wife wasn't a bad person; they just didn't speak the same language anymore. Maybe never did.

Well, that wasn't accurate. He must have cared for her once. The snow globe she gave him of the Washington Monument was still on his desk at school. It had, he thought, been his good luck charm and inspired his writing. Recently, less snow swirled each time he shook it, as if imitating the steady deterioration of their marriage. Now the marriage was toxic. Remaining in it would make him sick—might even, according to an article he'd read about stress, bring on cancer or shorten his life in another way.

Perhaps in his travels he would find someone, begin a new life. A professor of literature, Adam admired F. Scott

Fitzgerald's work, but he was determined to disprove his notion that "There are no second acts in American lives." Hopefully, out West the curtain might be raised on his own second act.

Americans have always headed West seeking new lives, but, so far, all Adam had experienced was dreary interstates, boredom, and loneliness. The first part of the trip, until Chicago, reminded him of New Jersey, and everything before the mountains looked like Iowa. Tourist attractions in the Midwest included a town famous for having the world's largest ball of string, a town where every summer they covered a large building with corn, and another town at the western extreme of South Dakota that advertised itself for five hundred miles with increasingly larger signs. The last billboard exclaimed "THIS IS IT!!!" It turned out the town offered nothing but a drug store with a giant souvenir department.

Souvenirs of what? Adam wondered. Why would anyone want a souvenir from this place? Nevertheless, thousands of the curious got off the interstate and stopped there each day, just as Adam couldn't resist doing, and bought ashtrays, pens, wall pennants, plaques, or bumper stickers with the town's name on them—as if this place deserved remembering. Most of these souvenirs would surely end up in garage sales and flea markets all over America and eventually in landfills. Of course, in a hundred years the few remaining ones might become "collectibles" worth a fortune, like old baseball cards.

He found himself thinking he would write a book some day on the entrepreneurial genius of places absent any distinction. Adam admired the sheer nerve of the South Dakota town, their *chutzpah*, using one of the few Yiddish words he knew, one that has no equal in English. His parents had spoken Yiddish only when they didn't want him to know what they were talking about.

Just beyond the South Dakota town were the Black Hills, and soon the Rockies were on the horizon. The landscape was improving, but not Adam's mood. He continued driving, observing little and thinking much, when late one afternoon he pulled into a parking lot at the South Rim of the Grand Canyon. Getting out of his car, he looked out over the canyon and its endless stone surroundings. It was as if he had landed on another planet. In the fading sun, the rock, now pink, had a soft, feminine quality.

It would be dark soon; he needed to find a place to stay. He had a pup tent with him but had already discovered that the nearby campground was full. He noticed a lodge just beyond the parking lot. Probably expensive, but a real bed would be worth it. He had slept in his car the night before in a highway rest area, stopping too late to find a campground or motel. All night he vacillated between keeping his windows open for air and closing them to shut out the mosquitos.

At four a.m. a policeman awakened him by tapping on the window with his nightstick. "No sleeping in rest areas," the cop said. There was just a hint of the coming day in the black sky as Adam drove off, exhausted and with a stiff neck. He wondered, what good was a rest area if you couldn't rest there? If all you could do in a rest area was use the toilet, why call them "rest areas?" Rest areas seemed vaguely reminiscent of those nothing places he was thinking of writing about, promising much but offering little. His wife had once found his literary musings attractive, but not recently.

In front of him on the check-in counter line stood a young woman with blond hair and a thick braid that hung down her back. Her khaki hiking shorts accentuated the roundness of her bottom. She had fine legs too. She looked like a hiker with low, well-worn and dusty hiking boots. When she momentarily turned to the side, he saw that she was also extraordinarily pretty, with sparkling eyes of an indeterminate color. Her tan polo shirt did nothing to disguise her breasts.

She looked like she was in her late twenties, maybe thirty. He hoped thirty or more. Since he was still thirty-nine, they would both be in their thirties; she wouldn't think he was too old for her. Sure, it was just a number, but…

He tried to quell his imaginings about the woman. She was probably here with a boyfriend, maybe a husband. A woman this beautiful certainly had men in her life, though perhaps she was traveling with a female friend. Was there a chance she was traveling alone? If so, might she be as eager as he for company? Unconsciously, he roughed up his hair to get more coverage. No question it was thinning on top, but no point advertising the fact.

She was at the counter now, and Adam overheard the clerk tell her, "Yep, there are rooms. Twenty dollars." Looking dispirited, the young woman started to move away. "Find someone to share the cost," the desk clerk called after her. "Two double beds in each room." But she didn't respond, just shook her head. Maybe this meant she was at the canyon alone.

Adam was torn. He was next in line. If he left his place, the last of the rooms might be taken, leaving him to sleep in his car in some remote area. Anxious some cop would bother him like the night before, he took the chance and went after the woman.

She had meandered into the gift shop and, in a desultory manner, was picking up various items and placing them back on the shelves: fossils, illustrated maps, books, and coffee mugs with pictures of the Grand Canyon. Better than the souvenirs at that glorified drugstore in South Dakota, but not by much. Adam would have been disappointed in the woman had she bought any of this junk, but he pretended to look at it too, eyeing her surreptitiously.

Finally summoning the courage, he approached her and said, "Excuse me." Startled, she turned, and Adam told her that he had been behind her in line at the check-in desk and gathered that she couldn't afford a room. He spoke rapidly, afraid she would cut him off at any time, given what he was proposing. Even if the results were negative, he needed to get it all said, to be sure he'd done his best. "I know this sounds unusual," he continued, "we're obviously strangers…I heard what the desk clerk said…about sharing a room…why don't we get a room—split the cost?…There's two double beds, so you can have one and me the other…I'm a nice guy, not crazy, perfectly normal…I won't bother you at all…I'm a professor." Adam thought telling her he was a professor might make him seem harmless enough.

He had gotten it all in, and he was certain this lovely creature would turn away without a word or say, *What do you take me for? Room with a perfect stranger?* But all she said was "Okay." Just like that, "Okay." Just like that he had a gorgeous roommate and a room at half price. He couldn't believe his luck.

"My name is Adam Levin," he said.

"Zoe Hildebrandt," she replied. Adam had always liked the name, Zoe. It connoted…well, he couldn't quite say what. Maybe a woman eager for adventure, willing to take chances. She started with an interesting name, so she probably was adventurous.

They shook hands. Her hand felt just right in his—the right size, soft, but with a firm grip. He didn't like when women limply shook hands, and he was required to do all the shaking. He liked when a woman met him halfway.

"Howdy, roommate," Adam said affecting a cowboy drawl. She smiled. It was a warm smile, and with it, her eyes flashed even more brightly, as if they carried an electric charge. "Howdy," she replied in a drawl of her own. She was a good sport; he could tell.

They went back to the check-in desk. Nobody was on the line, and Adam feared this meant no more rooms. But there were rooms, one anyway, so they each plunked down ten dollars and received plastic keys. Out in the parking lot they came upon Zoe's car—a green Pontiac, new and shiny as she was. It was parked right next to

They also talked about music, comparing the relative merits of the Beatles and the Rolling Stones. Zoe thought the Beatles were sweeter, the Rolling Stones more bitter.

"Which do you prefer?" Adam asked.

"Depends on where I am in my personal life, I guess," she replied. That was precisely what Adam was wondering: just where this incredibly attractive woman was in her personal life.

He was pleased that Zoe was a Bruce Springsteen fan. "Pure Jersey," Adam said proudly, adding that he had written a magazine story on Springsteen. Couldn't hurt for her to know he was a writer.

"I like New Jersey," she said.

"When were you there?" Adam asked.

"I haven't. But I like its energy. Everything seems to happen there."

They agreed that the Vietnam War had been a disaster. "At least we finally got rid of that scumbag Nixon last summer," Adam said.

"A hateful man," Zoe agreed. The two seemed to be in synch about everything. Adam was attracted to her not only physically but intellectually as well. Could she be his future?

She asked Adam about his writing.

Adam talked at length about his most recently published book, a novel—then realized that, in his eagerness, he had been doing most of the talking, a professorial affliction. Zoe was, by comparison, quiet, reticent—but definitely there. He vowed to encourage her to tell him things about herself by greater silence on his part. "I talk too much," he said.

"You're an interesting man," she said. "Tell me more about your writing."

Forgetting his resolution, Adam complied. He told her about his thoughts in South Dakota about a book titled *America's Nothing Places*. As he spoke, he noticed Zoe's generous lips. No lipstick, but she was so naturally lovely she didn't need any. He thought of what it would be like to kiss her.

Changing the subject, he volunteered that he was in the process of getting a divorce, thinking it wouldn't hurt for her to know that he was available. Zoe said nothing about her own availability, just that she was traveling in a rented car across the western United States by herself for the second time; she loved the American West.

It occurred to Adam that she did have a slight accent he couldn't place. "Where are you from, Canada?" He thought she might be French Canadian.

"No, Europe," she replied.

He vaguely noticed that she had said Europe but not which country. Probably one of the Scandinavian countries he imagined. She was certainly European: she held her knife and fork, each in one hand, never putting the knife down and switching the fork to her right hand in that robotic, almost military, way Americans eat. But what if she was German? Many of them spoke English perfectly. He was a little worried about that last name: Hildebrandt. It had a Germanic sound. No, she couldn't be German because...Well, just because. "But you have almost no accent," he said.

"As a child I went to the American School. Some of my best friends are Americans living abroad—*expats* I think you call them." Then she quickly added, "You've been kind to tell me about yourself and your writing. I can't wait to read a book of yours. But there's something you must know about me."

"I'm all ears," Adam said, eager to know not just something but everything about this woman. It was bound to draw them closer.

What she said had the exact opposite effect. "I am a lesbian," she said quietly. "I wanted you to know before we went back to our room, so there would be no misunderstanding."

Adam stared and tried to hide his disbelief and disappointment. "Fine," he quickly said in a magnanimous tone, "absolutely fine. But I'm glad you told me. I *am* very attracted to you."

"I could feel that coming off you; that's why I told you. No, what you Americans call, funny business when we get back to the room, okay?"

"Promise," he said.

"Just roommates?" she said with the hint of a smile.

"Absolutely," he replied affably, reaching across the table to shake hands with her again.

Inside he was laughing bitterly at himself. He had been calculating at what point he would make a move. Not here in the restaurant: too soon. Back in the room, certainly. Perhaps he would take her hand as they walked back to the room. And now he had indeed touched her hand again, but it was almost in a kind of farewell.

Oh well, Adam thought, trying to rationalize away his unhappiness. He never knowingly had a lesbian friend, not to mention roommate; it would be a new experience. It would also be nice to have the company, and he saved ten bucks. Still, he wondered whether it would be torture being alone with this beautiful woman in their room, lesbian or not, and trying to shut out all his libidinous thoughts and cravings.

He had been with other women as his relationship with his wife became more and more hopeless—being a professor at a university provided endless opportunities. But none of those other women had been remotely as attractive as Zoe. Not just her looks—everything.

What a disaster that she was a lesbian! How could she be a lesbian? She was the most beautiful woman he had ever been with. Okay, he had heard that being a lesbian had nothing to do with someone's looks; there were beautiful, sexy, very feminine women who were lesbians. "Lipstick lesbians," someone said. But lesbian or not, every move Zoe made, every gesture, everything about her was attractive to Adam. Maybe this lesbian thing was just her way of telling him she didn't want to sleep with him when they got back to the room. Well, he thought, maybe she'll change her mind, and if not, she's still wonderful to look at.

Back in the room they discussed watching television from their respective beds after taking showers. "You can go first," Zoe said.

Adam took fresh jeans and a blue polo shirt with him into the bathroom and, after showering, changed. Coming out of the bathroom barefoot, he sat on the side of his bed and read the television instructions, playing with the set mounted on the wall to see if he could get it going. Zoe went into the bathroom.

Fifteen minutes later she came out of the shower wearing nothing, as far as Adam could tell, but a large towel. What was up with that? he wondered. He really wondered when she sat down next to him on his bed. She smelled good. Was it perfume or the soap—or was this just how she smelled? What was he supposed to do? She had told him she was a lesbian. She had made him promise "no funny business." What was sitting on his bed in nothing but a towel if not funny business?

Adam put the television instructions down and sat on his hands; he had to do something with them. He wanted to put his arm around her, kiss her, but he had promised not to. His toes seemed to be curling up of their own volition. He hummed a tune, half overcome by desire, half paralyzed with fear that he might be misinterpreting her. Whatever happened, he didn't want to screw up.

Finally, mostly just to break the silence, he said, "I've got a little grass. Want to smoke a joint?" He assumed she would say no.

"Love to," she cried. She almost seemed high already in anticipation. In the Sixties, hippies smoked grass; now everyone did. Ordinary, middle class people, Adam included, were smoking dope. They were having their Sixties in the Seventies.

Besides, Adam had long thought the Sixties didn't begin until 1965 when the Vietnam War and opposition to it got going in earnest and civil rights became everybody's business. And there was Woodstock and the sexual revolution. John Kennedy had been assassinated in 1963, but it didn't initiate the Sixties—it brought Americans together. Now in the Seventies, the counterculture spawned in the late Sixties was becoming the culture and the old culture was in full retreat.

After two tokes each, Zoe's towel was off, Adam's clothes were on the floor, and a marathon of lovemaking began. They kissed—at first tentatively, then wildly. Her lips were just as luscious as he had thought. She pushed him down on the bed and rubbed her breasts across his face. He turned her over and caressed her bottom. It was as womanly as he had imagined it in her hiking shorts. He kissed it in appreciation. She turned and reached for his throbbing penis. "I want you in me," she said. She pushed him back in a shy, feminine way and sat on him, guiding his penis inside her. Touching herself while looking right at him with those eyes of hers, she kept gasping and then came, shuddering and screaming. She collapsed on him and he held her.

Adam had never been with such a passionate woman. He was thrilled. He started to kiss her again—her lips, her breasts. He went down on her and, in a short time, she was shuddering and screaming again.

It was quiet for a moment. "You're a wonderful lover," she said, something his wife had never told him.

Truthfully, he had never been a wonderful lover with his wife. She didn't have orgasms, and that—at least according to her—was Adam's fault. They couldn't even have a child. According to the doctors there was nothing the matter with her and both of them were fertile, but something about them, right down to her egg and his sperm, didn't connect. It was as if her egg saw his sperm coming and ran for its life.

Actually, after many tries, she did get pregnant twice but miscarried each time within a month. They gave up after that. They had less and less sex. Then none at all. What was the point? Sex had become fraught with tension, a difficult project on which they worked rather than played. They even went to a sex therapist for a year, but it did no good. And as their sexual connection faded so did their relationship in general.

In contrast, the lovemaking with Zoe was natural, easy, effortless. It went on—seemingly for hours. They gorged on each other. Was it some magical power of the Grand Canyon making all this happen? Inside her now, with Zoe urging him on, her hands on his back pulling him deeper into her, Adam felt like he was fucking the Grand Canyon. He was falling, falling…When he came it was as if his whole body exploded into its depths.

It hadn't just happened in his groin. He had felt it in his heart, in his lungs, in his whole body. It was sex as he had never experienced it before. So powerful, he thought it capable of either killing you or curing whatever ailed you. If you had cholesterol deposits, blockages even, they would be blown out of your arteries. "Jeez," he gasped.

As his breathing slowed, Zoe joked, "In what subject are you a professor, sex?"

Adam laughed. "Until now I was only a student."

Why had Zoe said she was a lesbian? Maybe because she hadn't yet decided she would come out of the shower wearing nothing but a towel or feared he might indeed be some kind of maniac, then decided otherwise. Was this her way of maintaining some control: saying "no" so as to later say "yes?" Women had their ways. Well, it didn't matter. Zoe was no more a lesbian than he was.

They fell asleep in Adam's bed wrapped around each other. In the middle of the night, this time in the dark, it started all over again. "Oh yes, oh yes, oh yes" she kept saying. She came again, and he did too, yelling her name, "Zoe, God!" If someone had told him that this lovely woman was indeed God, he would have believed it. He certainly was prepared to worship her. He already did worship her. They drifted off to sleep again.

CHAPTER 2

In the morning they woke up in her bed, though Adam had no memory of having moved there. They showered together, laughing and soaping each other, and then went to have breakfast in the restaurant. They got the same table—it had become *their* table—and sat looking out at the canyon, now salmon colored, deepening in color as the sun rose higher. "I'm in love with the canyon," Zoe said.

"I think I'm in love with you," Adam replied.

She smiled. This woman absolutely charmed him. She was beautiful and, at the same time, seemed so wise, so knowing. As at dinner the night before, they talked about everything, and now that they were lovers, the conversation took on greater importance for Adam. He noted that they laughed at the same things and were in synch about everything—out of bed and in.

Although neither had planned to stay more than one night at the canyon, after breakfast they went to the office and booked their room for another night. Zoe had a flight out of Phoenix in two days but would curtail her plans to see Indian ruins en route. "You're a lot livelier than any ruin," she said.

"I was a bit of a ruin before I met you," he replied. She gave him that wonderful smile.

Holding hands and stopping occasionally to kiss, they walked along the lip of the canyon, drinking in its immensity, its rugged vast beauty, and the salmon-colored rock highlighted by a perfect azure sky. Zoe added an even more powerful element; Adam could hardly imagine the sky and the rock without her. They made each other more beautiful.

They discovered a narrow, zigzagging path leading down into the canyon—lots of switchbacks—and hiked for an hour single file. Hugging the side of the canyon wall on their right, they were careful not to skid on the pink sand and pebbles that littered the trail. The left side of the trail was open, no barrier. If you went off there, you died.

The path reminded Adam of their lovemaking. Nothing cautious about either—both, all or nothing. He thought if you risk everything, you might just get everything. And now he had everything. He had never felt so alive.

Zoe led the way. He worried about her scraping her shoulder on the rock wall. She was his woman now; he would feel responsible if she got hurt—but she walked deliberately. Adam liked looking at her behind and legs and her shirt wet between her shoulder blades. When they stopped to rest at what proved to be their turn-around point, Adam put his arms around her and, pulling her towards him, licked the sweat on her neck. She giggled and pulled his hands down onto her breasts.

Adam read somewhere that the Navahos considered the Grand Canyon a holy place. One didn't just admire its beauty—one communicated with the Great Spirit. For sure, he and Zoe were not trampling on Indian sensibilities; their feelings for one another were the Great Spirit.

They sat on a boulder that half blocked the path. It must have broken off the rock wall centuries ago because it was weathered on all sides. While lunching on trail mix they had purchased at the restaurant checkout counter, they drank the water in their canteens.

"I have to pee," Zoe said. "Turn your back." Adam did as he was told, though he wouldn't have minded in the least to watch her. Every intimacy with her had a delicious quality.

He turned away and, opening his pants, sprayed the rock wall, his urine running down onto the sandy trail. Everything was a pleasure now—even just peeing out of doors. "Watch out below," he called to Zoe as he laboriously buttoned up his jeans.

In a moment she said, "You can turn around now." She was zipping up her shorts. Even that she did gracefully. His urine had run right into the puddle of hers that had pooled in a flat spot.

"Symbolic, no?" he said.

"Very," she said. "We've marked our territory."

"They're going to put an historical plaque on the rock: ZOE AND ADAM PEED HERE, 1975."

By late afternoon they were back in the room, comparing the tans they had acquired on the trail. Adam loved where Zoe's tan stopped below her neck, making her perfect white breasts seem exquisitely vulnerable, her nipples pinker. He wished he could someday watch her nurse a baby, their baby. But right now, her breasts belonged to him.

They showered together again and, still half wet, moved to one of the beds. "You have a very nice penis," Zoe said, taking hold of it gently. "And circumcised; I'm glad. Otherwise, a man looks like a horse."

"My tribe has come up with a few good ideas."

"I thought you might be Jewish. I often think of becoming a Jew. I once volunteered on a kibbutz in Israel for three months. Right now, I'm nothing, but I think I'd like to be a Jew. I'd be proud to join that fraternity: Einstein, Freud, even Jesus. And all the important feminists—Betty Friedan, Gloria Steinem…"

"Yeah, we Jews produce a lot of creative neurotics."

"And they produced you," she continued, "only you're not neurotic."

"Maybe I'd be more creative if I was. There's a guy at my university who's considered a genius. Nobel Prize material. He occasionally walks out of his office stark naked, and the departmental secretaries have to escort him back inside. He's also a dumpster diver and emerges with bits of garbage proving, he says, a theory of his about matter."

"Well," she said, laughing, "you're creative enough for me." She kissed him and the lovemaking started all over again. The grass the night before had broken down any barriers between them. Now there were no barriers to surmount. Their lovemaking just happened—smooth, easy.

Later, having come up for air, they said simultaneously "I'm starving" and laughed. Their stomachs as much as their minds and imaginations seemed to be in tune. They left their room for the restaurant and had the same waiter at their familiar table where they talked and laughed and laughed and talked. Adam again ordered what Zoe did. This time on purpose. "I want to be tasting just what you're tasting," he said.

He thought he had never been so happy. Why couldn't life always be this way—a perpetual celebration? Even food tasted better when he was with her.

While they were enjoying dessert, Zoe pointed out the window and said, "Look at that." Coming over the horizon was a huge black cloud. It grew as it advanced, now encompassing the whole sky. There seemed to be great turbulence welling up from within, smoky tendrils swirling down like snakes. Now there were hints of green and purple in the black—a frightening sky but with its own beauty, so different from the solid blue skies of the day. Now there was lightning. It didn't just light up the sky; bolts came crashing down on the rocks as if thrown by Zeus himself. You could see where it hit on the other side of the canyon, and now on the canyon wall itself. A bolt cleaved off a huge chunk of rock that went tumbling down into the gorge. It was thrilling: they had observed a geological event.

The massive weather was closer. The thunder, which normally comes seconds later, immediately followed the lightning. "We'd better go before this hits," Adam said.

But it already had. Outside, the temperature had dropped precipitously, and freezing rain was pouring down. "Let's run," Adam said, taking Zoe's hand. Now there was hail, and they were occasionally struck before making it through the parking lot to their room where, yanking open the door against the wind, they fell in onto the rough carpet and rolled about, laughing.

"I got bopped on the head a couple of times," Adam said.

"Me too." That started them laughing again. Adam thought he could lie there on the carpet forever laughing with this beautiful woman. And, quite apart from her beauty, had he ever felt so close to anyone?

"That kind of hail kills cattle in the fields."

"I feel sorry for the cattle," Zoe replied, "but ice crashing down from the sky has great drama. It's like an opera."

The menace of the storm made being alive and together more special than ever. It was as if they had defeated its power together. Now the room, so ordinary, seemed to glow. Even the pictures had mysteriously improved. Had others been substituted? Whatever, the pictures now were his and Zoe's and seemed to have an inherent beauty.

Finally, they got to their feet, removed their wet clothes, and climbed into a warm bath. Later, their lovemaking, in its intensity, seemed to echo the ferocity of the wind rattling the windows and the hail smashing against the roof.

In the morning they looked out on a dazzling scene of hail melting in the hot sun, some pieces as big as golf balls. Crunching across the parking lot hand in hand, they decided to spend yet another night together. Zoe would pass up the Indian ruins entirely. Awakening early the following day, she would drive straight to Phoenix Airport to catch her night flight to Europe.

Adam was joyful that he would have another day and night with Zoe at the canyon and in their room. Life was simple: hikes in the canyon, lovemaking in the room, and wonderful conversation in the restaurant. The restaurant was their restaurant, the table their table, and the room their room, as if they all had a permanent place in their lives.

They went to book the room.

"You two again?" the desk clerk said, laughing. "I didn't know I was running a matchmaking service."

"A very good one," Adam said. He insisted on paying the twenty dollars for the room himself this time.

"You don't have to do that," Zoe said.

"I want to," he replied. And then, lowering his voice, he said, "I want to take care of you. Indulge me. You bring out the old-fashioned gentleman in me."

"Well," she whispered as the desk clerk fussed with the paperwork, "you are gentle and *definitely* a man; I can testify to that. I don't know about old fashioned though."

They spent that morning like the previous one, hiking—but on a much wider trail their waiter told them about during breakfast—descending deeper into the canyon this time. When they stopped for their trail mix lunch, people passed by on sure-footed donkeys that left an animal stink in their wake, but that was okay. Everything was okay.

The people on the donkeys were descending to the Colorado River, a muddy trickle far below. Adam would have liked to follow them there but hiking back up in the heat would be exhausting and perilous without a lot more water.

In the afternoon another delightful shower, another extended bout of lovemaking.

"I love giving myself to you," Zoe said. "I love taking you too."

"Take all you want," Adam said.

"I'm so glad your name is Adam. You make me feel like Eve. And this is our Garden of Eden."

"Amen to that," Adam said.

In the restaurant for dinner they discovered that their table was taken. Adam was angry. How could anyone take their table?

"It doesn't matter," Zoe said.

"You're right," he agreed, but not having that particular table for their last meal together felt like a tiny flaw in their happiness. Later he would see it as foreshadowing things to come.

CHAPTER 3

A t dinner, Adam said, "This is getting serious, Zoe. Before we fall into each other's arms back at the room—as you know we will—I want to talk. I want to know all about you."

"I'm not sure that's a good idea," Zoe said. "Why can't we just go on as we are? This is our last night. Let's spend it immersed in the wonderful mystery of us."

"That's just the point," Adam said. "I don't want this to be our last night." He hesitated. The waiter, a different one than before, was asking for their orders. This time Adam looked at the menu and ordered something different from what Zoe ordered. This moment—different meals, different waiter—further foreshadowed things to come.

After the waiter took their orders and headed for the kitchen, Adam said, "Mystery is fine, but I want more. Much more. I know we met just over two days ago, but here I am thinking I want to marry this woman, have children with her, and I know so little about her.

"I want to know everything," he continued. "Where do you come from? What do you do for a living? Tell me about your family. As soon as possible I want to fly over and see you and make plans for the future. At first, maybe a long-distance relationship. But, later, you can move to America or I'll get a job there. Whatever, as long as we're together."

Zoe looked stricken.

"What's the matter?" Adam asked.

"After this night, we will never see each other again!" she said, staring at him intently, tears in her eyes.

Adam was shocked into silence. It was as if he had been hit with a club.

"You're kidding," he finally said.

"I'm afraid not," she replied.

"Why?!" he finally said, almost screaming. Other diners turned to look at them. "We're perfect for each other—intellectually, emotionally, sexually—the works. Do you have a husband back in, back in…" He realized that he still didn't know where in Europe she was from.

"I'm not married," she said, drying her tears with her paper napkin.

"Then?"

"I told you—I am a lesbian."

"That's ridiculous," he said.

"Ridiculous that I am a lesbian? Don't you think that's insulting?"

"I mean ridiculous that you *think* you're a lesbian."

"But I am," she insisted firmly "That's why I can never see you again. Annika and I do not keep secrets from each other. But this, with you…it would break her heart. I may keep it to myself, not just because of her but to savor it quietly over the years: this wonderful thing that happened to me at the Grand Canyon. How could

I share this with anybody but you? Maybe someday we will see each other again—even if it's twenty years from now—and we'll reminisce about these days."

Adam was incredulous. "I thought you made up the lesbian thing to keep me at a distance 'til you were sure of me. Now you say it's for real? It can't be. This thing between us, this chemistry—it isn't just happening to me, is it?"

"It's was just as wonderful for me," she said.

"Was?"

"Is! We have another night together. Let's not spoil it now."

Adam persisted. "Well, if it's wonderful for you, how can you be a lesbian? You're at least bisexual."

"The me you know is not who I am…normally. Twice I was with men before Annika, but it was no good. I was even married for a year."

"How'd that work out?"

"Badly," she said, almost grimacing. "Nothing like this with you. This was magic. I don't know what came over me here at the canyon."

"What came over you?!" Adam flashed angrily. "What was I, a novelty, a heterosexual fling?"

Again, the other diners turned in their direction. A man got up and walked over to their table. "Why don't you two take this outside?" he suggested.

Adam surprised himself. The man was much bigger than him, but Adam said, in his most menacing tone, unconcerned about the consequences, "Shut the fuck up and mind your own damn business!" The man hesitated for a moment, then walked away, shaking his head.

"No, not a novelty, not a fling," Zoe continued. "When I came out of the shower in a towel, I was thinking, why not an adventure? But almost at once I began to care deeply for you. And now…You will always be with me—the only man I ever loved."

"That's complimentary," Adam said, "but I don't buy it. I've never been with a woman who was so sexual. And I mean man-woman sexual. You say you're a lesbian. I don't know anything about that. For me, you're magnificently heterosexual. I've never had feelings for a woman like those I have for you."

"But," he continued, "what about you? All that passion, all that screaming—was it some show you were putting on? Were you faking it all along?"

"I would like to believe I have never faked anything in my life," Zoe said. "No, every moment was real. You made me feel wonderful. Not just in bed—on our hikes, eating together, our talks. I didn't know I could feel this way with a man."

"Then maybe you've discovered who you really are. Maybe this lesbian thing is an illusion, Zoe. I'm not going to let this be just an adventure. I told you earlier that I think I'm in love with you. Now, I'm taking away the I think. For Chrissake, if you're a lesbian, then I'm crazy."

"I *am* a lesbian, but you're not crazy. I completely let myself go with you. I loved you just as you loved me. Not just with my body, with my soul. But it has to end here at the Grand Canyon."

"I'd sooner jump into the canyon than give you up," he shouted. The man at the other table started to get up again, but his wife said something to him, and he sat back down, glaring in their direction.

For a long time, they sat silently, picking at their food, not meeting each other's eyes. Adam felt a profound sense of loss; he didn't know whether to be furious or cry. He had met the love of his life, and she insisted she was a lesbian. He had gone from loneliness to ecstasy to agony in little more than forty-eight hours. A rare and beautiful butterfly had blossomed into life and, after briefly fluttering its wings, had died.

He wouldn't let it die. "Look," he said, "there are heterosexuals, homosexuals, bisexuals, and now I hear there are even transsexuals. But there aren't lesbians who make passionate love with men. If they do, they're bisexuals, damn it. Unless they're crazy, schizophrenic maybe, two different people."

"I don't understand it either," Zoe responded, "but I am one person; I am a lesbian; I am not bisexual. It took me a long time to learn this."

"What someone is, is what they do," Adam rejoined.

"What they normally do," Zoe said. "Please, Adam, this was so beautiful. Don't spoil it now." Things went silent again.

Finally, Adam said, "Tell me about you. If all I'm going to be left with is a memory, I want to know where you live so I can picture you somewhere, so I can follow the news there. I want to know about your family, where you went to school, what you do for a living—anything you can tell me will make it easier for me. Otherwise, I'll begin to think I imagined all this, that it never happened, that everything at the Grand Canyon was a hallucination."

She sat in silence for a while, looking down at the table. Finally, she said, "I am German. I am a lawyer. I studied at the Free University of Berlin. Annika and I live in West Berlin next to the wall. My mother lives in the capital of West Germany, Bonn, where I grew up."

Oh shit, Adam thought. Earlier he dismissed the idea that Zoe could be German. He had met American women with the name Zoe. He thought a German woman would have a name like Brunhilde, a hard name, a name that made her sound like she had been a sadistic guard in a concentration camp. Had he really fallen in love with a German?

Furthermore, he wasn't just in love with a German; he was in love with a lesbian. A fucking lesbian kraut. From Berlin, no less.

He hated the very word. Berlin. It stood for everything evil in the world. He wished there wasn't a town in New Jersey named Berlin. And then there was Irving Berlin, a Jew who wrote "White Christmas" and "Easter Parade." It was fine that he wrote songs for Christians—some of them sing the songs but hate Jews anyway. But wouldn't an "Irving," a typical Jewish name, feel uncomfortable with the last name "Berlin?"

"I can't believe you're German," Adam said, flatly.

"But I am. And you must never try to find me," Zoe continued, "never look for me in Berlin."

"I thought you might be Norwegian or something. "So many of them speak English perfectly too." Adam had once lectured in Oslo. At an idle moment he had imagined Zoe as a descendant of the heroic Norwegian resistance fighters, ambushing their Nazi occupiers and, in their white parkas and pants, blending into the snow as they escaped over the mountains on skis.

"No, I am German."

"Oh, shit!" Adam said.

"Why oh shit?"

"Because I hate Germans!" he shouted, again startling the people at that nearby table and others further across the dining room.

"You hate me?"

He didn't answer. He wasn't sure whether he wished to wound Zoe because she was German or insisted she was a lesbian after causing him to fall in love with her or both. He felt like someone who had discovered a great treasure, and now it was being taken away from him on technicalities.

"I thought from the beginning you might feel that way," she said, her face reddening. "Other Americans do, not just Jews. Only a generation has passed. How do your students feel about Germans?"

"They're different from me," Adam said reluctantly. "Even the Jewish ones. For them the Holocaust is history. For me it's still *now.*"

"That's why I said 'European' when we met. You hate the Nazis, so do I. But hating all Germans, perhaps forever? That's insane. Hating me makes no more sense than me hating you because of African slavery or because of the slaughter of the Indians or because you Americans stole half of Mexico to extend slavery in what you proudly call the Mexican War. To this day your Marines sing 'From the Halls of Montezuma,' celebrating their crimes."

"I had nothing to do with slavery or the Indians or Mexico. Nor did anyone in my family. My grandparents emigrated to America years after all that."

"And you think I had something to do with the Nazis? I was a tiny infant when the war ended."

"What about your father? Was he in the German army? Was he a Nazi?"

"I have no father," she answered angrily.

"Everyone has a father."

"No, my mother lived just this side of the Polish border and at age sixteen was gang raped twice by Russian soldiers as they advanced on Berlin. Probably eight of them the first time and five more later. She lost count. She never trusted men after that and never married.

"The sperm of one of those rapists was my father," she continued, heatedly. "That's all I have for a father, some Russian rapist's sperm. And if you're going to hate Germans, don't I have good reason to hate Russians? I hate the rapists, but I don't hate Russians—certainly not as you hate Germans.

"Jews do not have a monopoly on suffering" she went on with a sigh. "The Nazis killed homosexuals and gypsies and liberals and anyone who didn't support them or pretend to. And look at what the Japanese did. They used the Chinese for bayonet practice, forced Korean women to be comfort women, and treated American prisoners of war like savages, worked them to death, tortured them, beheaded them. And they never apologized. Never.

"We did. We keep putting up memorials; every year more. We have this word, *Vergangenheitsbewältiguug*, which roughly means working through the past, never ignoring it.

"The Japanese do ignore their past, which was as ugly as ours. Were the Japanese more humane because they didn't single out Jews for mistreatment and death? Is one human being more important than another?"

He knew what Zoe had said was true, and it made him uncomfortable, not just about the Japanese. He had lectured in Japan several years before and didn't once think about Japanese atrocities in the 1930s and during World War II. Pearl Harbor never crossed his mind. He had enjoyed Japan, liked his Japanese hosts, loved Japanese food.

"I'm sorry for what happened to your mother," he said. But deep down, part of him still thought all Germans had it coming: Dresden firebombed, widespread starvation, millions of soldiers and civilians dead, women raped. They deserved it all. There were no innocent Germans. They were a race of monsters.

CHAPTER 4

He thought he might try a more neutral topic. "Tell me, how did you get your name, Zoe?' It doesn't sound like a German name."

"As the war was ending, my mother moved to the American zone to get away from the Russians. An American soldier, seeing that she was pregnant and starving, gave her a chocolate bar. He told her that she reminded him of his sister Zoe and told her that Zoe in Greek means *life*."

"You were born in 1945. What month?"

"April."

"That's weird. My wife—ex-wife, whatever—was born that April."

"What is her name?"

"I'm trying to totally forget her. Her name alone makes me ill when it doesn't make me angry."

"Still," Zoe said, smiling, "you seem to have a fixation on women born in April 1945." Adam tried to smile as well.

"In any case, if you hold me responsible for what the Nazis did to the Jews, there's nothing I can do. Most Germans were evil then, but today, we're pretty good people. Open-minded, creative. And we were that way before the

Nazis too. Great artists of all kinds: Beethoven, Bach, Brahms, Goethe, Schiller, the Bauhaus, the Expressionist painters."

"I'll never trust Germans," he insisted, his rage returning.

"And even during the Nazi period, there were good Germans who risked their lives to save Jews. If they got caught, they were hung. Other good Germans opposed the Nazis and were sent to concentration camps. Don't you know that?"

"I do," he said, "but only in my head. My blood boils when I think of Germans; it's in my DNA. For me, Germans and Nazis are one and the same. Anyone with a 'Von' before their last name I especially don't trust because then I know they're German."

"That's ridiculous. Von just means there was once nobility in the family—maybe centuries ago. There were German Jews with von before their names. The Jewish-American film director, Josef von Sternberg, wasn't a von when he was born in Germany. He put it on when he got to Hollywood to give himself some class. What about the von Trapps? They hated the Nazis and escaped from Austria. Do you have something against *The Sound of Music* because it's focused on a family with von before their name?"

"Whatever," Adam said, not wanting to hear this. "As a boy I dreamed of machine-gunning Nazis, strangling them with my bare hands. I've been all over the world but have never set foot in Germany and never will. When I fly overseas, I make sure never to change planes in

German airports. I've never owned a German car. Volkswagen Beetles aren't cute for me; they make me think of Hitler and his 'Volk.' I don't buy anything that says, 'Made in Germany.' A month ago, I discovered that a pair of scissors I've had for years had 'Made in Germany' stamped into the steel. I threw it in the garbage can."

"That's crazy," Zoe said hotly. "American Jews and Israelis visit West Germany. Some buy a Mercedes or a BMW while there. Last month, the Israeli Prime Minister visited Germany. Besides, what do German cars or scissors or airports have to do with Nazis and Jews? Annika and I are thinking of becoming Jewish because we see Jews as enlightened, not as bigots. When Nazi Germany killed German Jews, it killed the best part of us—our artists, our musicians, our writers, our intellectuals, and many of our Jewish patriots who distinguished themselves in World War I. It wasn't just murder; it was suicide. We hate the Nazis as much—no, more—than you do. They make us ashamed to be German. We feel responsible for them. You don't have to."

But Adam was hardly listening. "Even the German language disgusts me when it doesn't terrorize me" he said. "*Actung, raus* and all that shit."

"That's probably because the only Germans in movies you have seen are Nazis shouting like the sadistic pigs they were."

"I'd hear people speaking Dutch or one of the Scandinavian languages and thought they might be speaking German and were Nazis," he said. "I'd even hear Jewish refugees speaking Yiddish, mostly German in origin I'm told, and think they were secret Nazis. German Jewish refugees had sons my age with names like Bruno and Karl with a *K* instead of a *C*. I avoided those kids."

"German is just a language like any other," she said. "Those are just names."

"Not to me," he replied angrily. "I don't even like that word Deutsche. Deutsche Bank—gives me the creeps."

"But that just means German bank. And I think it was founded by Jews."

The waiter arrived with the dessert list. Adam waved him off. Dessert was celebratory. The last thing he felt like doing right now was celebrating.

"You seem as prejudiced against Germans as they were against Jews," Zoe said with fervor. "It's a sickness in you, an obsession. You have Hitler on the brain. It's as if you need him to explain all of the evil in the world. You're *married* to him—like two pieces of wood joined by a carpenter."

"Married to him? Give me a break!" He stared down at his food for a long time. Finally, he said, "It may take generations until Jews can stop looking over their shoulders and be normal. This may be a sickness, but it's one I don't expect to recover from."

"You mean you don't want to recover from it? And don't you think Germans today want to be normal too?"

Adam was aware they were talking at cross purposes, but he didn't care. "Some Jews say, 'Forgive, but never forget.' I say, 'Never forgive, never forget.'"

"That's okay. But it's not okay to keep Hitler and the Nazis alive the way you do. It's pathological. Hitler is dead, forever dead!"

"Maybe for everyone but the Jews. For me, Hitler and the Holocaust aren't the past. Who knows when those beasts may start up again? There are six million Jews in America and six in Israel. A new generation of Nazis would have choices if killing six million Jews was their thing."

"If there is one country that will never have Nazis again it is Germany," she said.

"Says who?" Adam replied irately.

"We have been inoculated. We know the evil we are capable of. Other countries do not know. Americans especially do not know. Look at the atrocities you committed in Vietnam. Americans were the Nazis at My Lai."

Things went silent again. Adam looked away. A little girl was staring at him over the tabletop where she was sitting with her family ten feet away. She stuck her tongue out at Adam. He wasn't amused.

Zoe asked, "Did you lose family in the Holocaust?"

"Distant relatives. I never knew any of them, but their framed pictures were on the wall in my grandparents' apartment." There had been old women with wigs, men with beards and yarmulkes, and children with dark, sad eyes. There was a boy around his age at the time who stood holding his father's hand. He must have been killed by the Nazis. Adam thought about that boy a lot; he could have been that boy. No one in the pictures was smiling. Maybe they had nothing to smile about because they would soon be murdered.

"They were the relatives who didn't emigrate to America," he told Zoe. "Some of them had died years before Hitler could get them. They were the lucky ones, my father said. He told me that my grandparents wrote for a time to those who were alive and they replied. My grandfather let me soak the Hitler stamps off the envelopes and put them into my stamp album. It horrifies me that I did that, saved stamps with the face of the man who was killing my people. I was too young; I knew little about him. And then the letters stopped coming. I never knew any of those relatives, not even their names.

"But nothing happened to me. The relatives in those pictures were ghosts. Europe, the war, was as far away as the moon. I was a safe little American boy."

"So now you have to make up for it? To pay a price as others did? It's as if you feel deficient because you don't have a number tattooed on your arm."

"Maybe. As a child I learned there were people who wanted to kill me just because I was a Jew. First the Holocaust and then Israel reborn and under threat ever since. But except for sending a check once in a while— this Jewish cause, that Jewish cause—I've sat high up in the stadium watching 'the real Jews' down on the field competing in deadly games against the bad guys. The least I can do is hate the Germans."

"Hate the Germans—and maybe hate yourself too. You should suffer because you haven't suffered? And you'd like to see Germans suffer, even people like me? Someone who was a tiny infant when the war ended? Someone who volunteered to work on a kibbutz in Israel? Someone who is thinking of becoming a Jew?"

Adam didn't know what to say in response to her. Finally, "What's the difference? Now you don't have to worry about me coming over to look for you in Berlin. I wouldn't give Germans the satisfaction of knowing I had spent a single day, a single penny, in their country."

"Or spent yourself more than once inside a German woman you said you were in love with."

That stopped Adam momentarily. "If I'd known you were German, maybe this wouldn't have happened," Adam said." I don't fuck just anybody."

Zoe winced. "Wouldn't want to get yourself dirty?" She looked hurt, and he thought he had gone too far.

"I'm lying," he said, taking her hand. "I don't feel dirty. I've never been with a woman and felt so wonderful." Nevertheless, it flashed across his brain that maybe the Germans had come up with a new way to torture Jews: get them to fall in love with German lesbians and then abandon them, leave them floating, untethered to their lives.

When Adam had married, it was axiomatic he would marry a Jewish girl. Two out of five Jews in the world had gone up in smoke, so the least he could do was to father Jewish children. You couldn't count on doing that if you married a non-Jewish woman, a *shiksa*.

But Zoe wasn't just a shiksa. She was a German lesbian shiksa. If he had looked the world over, he couldn't have found a woman offering a less promising résumé. His wife, straight and Jewish—and a professor like himself—had the perfect résumé for him but was an impossible woman. The irony appalled him. His marriage to the "right kind of woman" hadn't worked, and here he was crazy about the "wrong kind of woman."

He knew of women who loved gay men and thought they could reform them. Some called them "fag hags." What was he? What did one call a man who falls in love with a woman who, it turns out, is a lesbian? He had once heard the term "lesbro." It apparently referred to men who, for sport, sought out lesbians in hopes of seducing them. Is that what he was? No, damn it, he hadn't fallen in love with Zoe because she was a lesbian but because she was the most desirable woman he had ever known and because he didn't believe, still couldn't believe, that she was a lesbian.

Perhaps he was just a fool or a participant in a cruel joke. A Jewish joke. *"Rabbi, I've fallen in love with a German lesbian shiksa"* would be the first line, but he didn't know where it would go from there. Perhaps the rabbi would say, in a Yiddish accent, *"The goyim know more than we do about fency fucking."*

Trying to think of a joke was the only mirth Adam would experience that evening. He and Zoe walked joylessly back to their room, side by side, not holding hands. They watched television sitcoms, the canned laughter mocking their silence, which seemed louder than the television. Adam didn't laugh once. It was torture. Everything that had been wonderful between them—the lovemaking, the emotions, the talk, the laughter—had died. After all of their intimacies, they were strangers, each hurting in their own bed.

Eventually, they turned off the television, put out the lights, and got under the covers of their respective beds without once touching, without a word. Half an hour later, desperate now, Adam called across to her in the dark: "Zoe, I don't care if you're German. I don't care if you're a lesbian." He cared immensely about these things, but not as much as he cared about losing her forever. He was in love with Zoe, and he had never been in love before. He must have briefly loved his wife, or thought he did, but he had never been *in* love with her.

He wanted Zoe, needed her. He didn't know in what capacity, but anything at all would be better—with her just three feet away—than the solitary, cold bed in which he now found himself.

Zoe mumbled something in her sleep, but he couldn't make it out. Despite his sorrow, he wished he was in bed with her. Even just holding her, nothing more. Some kind of goodbye if there had to be a goodbye. He thought of just getting into her bed, sleeping with his arms around her. She would probably welcome that. But if there was no future with Zoe, he might as well start mourning her loss now. Getting into her bed would give him even more to grieve about, to recover from, and make it worse in the long run.

When Adam awoke in the morning, Zoe wasn't there. He stumbled to the front of the room and, parting the vertical blinds, looked out. Her car was gone. How was it that the sounds of her leaving hadn't awakened him? Perhaps it was because he had nothing to wake up for.

In the bathroom he discovered that she had written a note in lipstick on the mirror:

IF YOU LOVE ME
NEVER TRY TO FIND ME.
BUT I WILL ALWAYS LOVE YOU.
YOU MUST BELIEVE THAT!

Adam was glad to see the note, but what good did it do him? He tried to rub it off with toilet paper. No point leaving it there for the chambermaid to see and know his shame, his horror. The red lipstick smeared, and he couldn't get it all off. In the mirror was his forlorn face, looking like it was enveloped in a cloud of blood.

Miserable, Adam wasn't sure what made him feel worse: the loss of Zoe or that the love of his life was a German lesbian. How had he screwed up so badly? Zoe might cause him to rethink his feelings about to-day's Germans—some of them, or at least her—but what could he possibly do about her being a lesbian?

Some of the lipstick was on his hand, but he wasn't in a hurry to get it off. It was like a wound, but it was all he had left of Zoe. "Oh, shit," he said quietly. Then he did something he hadn't done in years. He began to cry.

CHAPTER 5

Adam put on the first clothes he could grab.

There was no point being neat. For what? For whom? He now looked as he did when he first arrived at the Grand Canyon—before taking a shower and changing his clothes and falling in love with Zoe. He looked the same but felt worse. Then he still had hope and hadn't yet experienced the greatest disappointment of his life. He just threw his things into his suitcase.

He went to his car and sat in it, without starting the motor. Where should he go? He sat there a long time, staring at his hands on the steering wheel, the same hands that once held Zoe.

Adam reached for the keys, dangling from the ignition, but since he did not know where he was going, he sat there thinking of the world in which he grew up: the Holocaust, World War II, and the rebirth of Israel. All of it fraught with horror or at least danger. His Uncle Jack had served in the US Army and was slightly wounded in the Battle of the Bulge. When the Germans were defeated, he was sent briefly to Poland and visited Auschwitz and saw the bodies stacked up. When he came home, he was sick—not bed sick—sick in the head. He told Adam, "Germans aren't people; they're a lower form of

life. I won't call them animals because that would be un-
fair to animals. Most animals only kill other animals to
eat. Germans kill just to kill, and they're all Nazis; don't
let anyone tell you different. We should have wiped them
out—every one of them. Soon they'll be back, and this
time they'll come after the rest of the Jews."

Uncle Jack was put in a psychiatric hospital. Adam's
parents said he was "depressed."

They gave him shock treatments, but they must have
used too much electricity because it stopped his heart.
"The Germans couldn't kill him in the war, but they got
him anyway," Adam's father would say.

In Jack's childhood, things were black or white, never
gray. Americans were the good guys, Germans the bad.
Hitler was perfect for a child's world of black or white, so
evil he was famous for it. Adam's father told him Hitler
was chosen as *Time Magazine's* Man of the Year for 1938,
and he had appeared regularly on magazine covers.

Hitler, Hitler, Hitler. Adam heard his name in his
Bronx apartment as often as he heard F.D.R. Hitler was
more important than God. God was a mystery; Hitler
was real. Growing up Jewish in those days, Adam felt like
he was on the endangered species list. To protect himself
while walking on the sidewalk, he made certain never to
step on a crack, though sometimes he switched and made
sure to step on every crack. When a car came down the
street, he would race it along the sidewalk to the corner.
Heaven knows what would have happened if he didn't
beat it. But he only allowed himself to beat it narrowly.
Beating it by a lot might have invited retribution from

Germany. But what if he tripped and fell racing to the corner? He tried not to think about it.

Now he sat silently in his car and thought about his life, his obsession with Hitler, and his relationship with Zoe. It wasn't so much the lesbian thing; it was the German thing. He still hoped the lesbian thing could change.

Was it possibly the German thing made him always put on his left sock first since childhood? It was like racing cars to the corner. Why the left and not the right sock? He couldn't say. But it seemed safer and kept Hitler away. He realized he did it today while getting dressed.

Without these rituals he believed something terrible would happen. Hitler's evil eye was watching his every move. He knew this was stupid—cracks in the sidewalk, socks, the evil eye—but it was real for him.

As a boy, walking around his neighborhood he was always careful to pick up scraps of print from Jewish newspapers. He didn't know the meaning of what was written, but anything in Hebrew print might be as precious as a piece of the Torah and had to be safeguarded. Not picking it up would be like stepping on Jewish graves. Who knew what the Nazis or even American anti-Semites would do with it if they got hold of it? He always put such litter in his jean pockets where he would find it several laundry days later rolled up like a spitball, the ink largely washed away.

Also, Adam and his neighborhood friends formed the "Hitler House Club." Once a week on Tuesdays immediately after school, they would gather at the edge of the vacant lot full of poison ivy and litter just behind the apartment building where many of them lived, including Adam's family. They had a cardboard box one of them had fished out of the garbage or obtained from his parents. A different boy was responsible each week for bringing a box and had the honor of carrying it.

One end of the Hitler box was open, the flaps free, and the other end was still sealed. They would puncture the center of the sealed side with a stick, the stick being Hitler. Sometimes they would add another stick or two for Mussolini and the Japanese general Tojo, but usually it was just Hitler.

When the five or six kids were assembled, Jimmy Schwartz would start playing his little toy drum, and they would march solemnly across the lot in single file. It had all the trappings of a military execution. The boy carrying the box, Hitler stick side up, placed it in a ring of large, now fire-blackened stones near their clubhouse. He would light a flap or two with matches. The boys were told by their parents not to play with matches, but they weren't playing—this was war. Soon the whole box was ablaze. As the flames crept up the box towards the Hitler stick, they watched expectantly. When the Hitler stick ignited like a torch, they would cheer, "Fuck you, Adolf. Up yours, Nazi pig."

They were somewhat chastened to learn that there was a great Jewish American basketball star whose name was Adolph Schayes. He was just a high school player then but known throughout the country. His first name was spelled differently, but what a terrible name to be born with, Adolph, especially for a Jew. The basketball star adopted the nickname "Dolph," and none of the boys ever mentioned his full first name. Dolph had been born before Hitler came to power. Now no Jewish family would name their child Adolph or Adolf. Maybe no one, anywhere, would give their child such a terrible name except Nazis; though, when one thought of it, it was just a name. Maybe, before Hitler, there were good Adolfs— even Jewish ones.

There was a German Jewish refugee boy in Adam's class who wanted to be part of their Hitler House Club, but his last name was Lipschitz, almost as unattractive a name as Adolph—but for different reasons. Lipschitz was like "stink bomb." The boys called him "Shitlip." His first name, Hans, didn't help. The boys didn't want any Krauts in the club, even Jewish Krauts. They held a formal vote to exclude Lipschitz. Of course, if he had been a great basketball player like Dolph Schayes, it might have been different, but he only played a weird, almost entirely foreign sport in those days, soccer—not baseball or football or basketball—and when he swam in the neighborhood pool, he only swam breaststroke, not crawl or freestyle, which was what real Americans swam.

Each box burning provided the boys an illusion of safety. This "Jewish voodoo," they trusted, was having its effect in Berlin. If it didn't kill Hitler, at least it would give him a headache or indigestion or make sure he had a bad day.

Burning Hitler and his house, the boys felt, helped the war effort. One fall, the fire from the burning box spread to the dry leaves around it, and then a gust of wind spread it to the dried patch of poison ivy that flourished around the base of the nearby oak tree. They managed to swat out the fire with their jackets but not before being enveloped in poison ivy smoke.

Adam awoke the next morning with his scalp, armpits, groin, chest, ears, and eyelids covered with red welts. His ears itched the most; they turned fiery red with the scratching. His mother painted his body pink with calamine lotion and made him wear mittens so he couldn't scratch. The other boys were also covered with poison ivy rashes; one ended up in the hospital. Hitler must have heard about the box ritual in the vacant lot and taken his revenge. The boys didn't burn a Hitler box for weeks afterwards.

Hitler could also be a source of fun. Sometimes Adam and his friends would take small pieces of broken black combs and hold them under their noses. They *Sieg Heiled* with their other arm and goose-stepped around the vacant lot. Ridiculing Hitler and the Nazis also contributed to the war effort they told themselves.

Another way was picking up discarded cigarette packs and stripping the tinfoil from the paper wrapping inside. The vacant lot was especially good for finding cigarette packs because people felt free to litter there. It was a no-man's land whose owner was unknown; it was never cleaned up. The boys would collect this thin metal, making a large ball of it. They gave it to Jimmy's father, who owned a junkyard, to help in the war effort.

You could do anything in the vacant lot, unlike the playground and park with their huge "NO" signs followed by the long list of things you couldn't do. The park was like the Bible: all "shalt nots." In the vacant lot you could have rock fights or snowball fights or make fires. Or you could have a clubhouse, as the boys did, made from a large wooden packing crate that had mysteriously appeared in the lot, probably dumped there by a moving company. For a while the boys kept two pigeons in the clubhouse. They would fly away, circle, and come back when they were hungry. But one day they flew away and never returned. The boys thought maybe hawks got them.

Adam also had his own little victory garden in another part of the vacant lot. He tried to grow vegetables to help the war effort, but the only thing that grew well was radishes. He didn't like radishes nor did his mother and father, but there was a neighbor in Apartment 2G, just below their apartment, Mrs. Schneiderman, who was always glad to take the radishes, even covered in dirt. "I'll wash them off, she assured Adam. "Thank you for helping America win the war against Hitler." She told him that his radishes would mean more radishes available for "our boys overseas." It made him proud.

Everyone was patriotic in those days. Adam would save up pennies, nickels, and dimes till he had enough to buy twenty-five cent Minute Man stamps and paste them up in a book. Over several years he also miraculously saved $18.75 from his tiny allowance and bought a $25 war bond with it. For years afterwards the figure $18.75 caused patriotic feelings to well up in him. He almost didn't want to cash in the bond after the war and get his $25.

CHAPTER 6

The most patriotic person in Adam's apartment building was Mr. Silverman, who lived on the first floor. He was the air raid warden. When the sirens sounded, Silverman was out in the street wearing his yellow helmet. He knew which windows went with which apartments and the names of the people who lived in those apartments throughout the six-story building. If you had a sliver of light coming through the dark curtains, he would yell up from the street, "Whats-a-matta with you Cohens up in 4F? You want the Nazis to kill us all with their bombs?" Even when there wasn't an air raid drill, Adam's mother on Friday nights, when she lit the Sabbath candles, covered the windows in the kitchen with black cloth in addition to the curtains. She believed Nazi bombs were designed to seek out apartments with Sabbath candles.

Silverman was the unofficial "mayor" of the building. Some years after the war he was the first to get a television set—as if his high station called for it. Everyone competed for an invitation to witness the miracle. On some evenings there would be twenty people in the Silverman's living room, sitting on plastic covered furniture looking at a screen not much bigger than a radio dial and with only one channel. Adam gave Silverman's son, who was his age, Superman and Batman comic books to occasionally gain entrance. At midnight the American flag occupied the screen, the "Star Spangled Banner" was played, and the set went dark. Adam and the other neighbors crept out quietly, whispering thank you as they returned to their apartments.

Like most people in the neighborhood, Silverman was Jewish. In fact, Adam grew up thinking almost everyone was Jewish. He was aware of people called Christians who worshipped a Jewish guy who got nailed to a cross. He never could understand why they had picked out this particular guy when, as he had heard, the Romans nailed hundreds, maybe thousands, of Jews to crosses, anybody who got out of line. Still, you had to feel sorry for that Jesus guy. He looked so sad in all the pictures. But how had Christians figured out what he looked like? They didn't have cameras back then. Maybe somebody drew a picture of him, Adam thought.

Christians also seemed to worship a red-faced tubby guy with a white beard who didn't seem to be Jewish like the Jesus guy. He went "Ho, ho, ho" all the time and lived up at the North Pole with a bunch of reindeer. He came around once a year with presents—but only for the Christians. It didn't seem fair. Jewish parents hustled to make up for it with Chanukah, eight days not just one.

Adam could never understand what the connection was between the tubby guy and the Jesus guy and which one was more important. Christians seemed to like the tubby guy more. They smiled when they talked about him, but looked serious, even grim, when discussing the Jesus guy.

Most of the teachers in Adam's elementary school were Christian, and most of the kids were Jewish. The Christian teachers made the Jewish kids sing Christmas carols every December as if they were doing them a favor by including them. "Silent Night" was pretty, though Adam never understood what "round yon virgin" meant. He asked his mother about the "virgin" part, but she said he'd learn about that when he was older. Well, he thought, if you weren't supposed to know about the virgin thing till you were older, how come kids were singing about it now? His mother had no idea what the "round yon" meant.

Christian stuff was, for Adam, strange, foreign, even dangerous. He had heard that Christians murdered Jews for centuries; then Hitler and the Nazis took over. He didn't want to be killed, so he sang Christian songs when the teachers made him. And this was long before fun songs like "Rudolph, the Red-Nosed Reindeer." One song that seemed strange was the one that ended with "...born is the King of Israel." Maybe Jesus was a nice guy, but he sure wasn't the King of Israel—that was David or Solomon, those guys.

Besides all the Christian and Hitler stuff he had to contend with, Adam's Jewish education had been strange. His parents took him to a synagogue inside a hospital only three blocks from their apartment called the Beth Abraham Home for the Incurables, where he also had his bar mitzvah training and, eventually, his bar mitzvah. The rabbi of the synagogue, who tutored Adam, had a long white beard that often displayed evidence of what he had eaten during the previous twenty-four hours. He would stroke his beard while teaching Adam, occasionally finding a morsel and placing it into an ashtray on his desk.

Most of the synagogue's congregation were patients of the hospital. They were frightening. Many had something wrong with their brains, a kind of sleeping sickness. They just sat there, never moved, or said anything—the expressions on their faces never changed.

Different kinds of "incurables" could be encountered in the synagogue. They staggered in like zombies or were rolled in on wheelchairs. Others came in on gurneys, lying face down, poling themselves with their two canes along the hospital corridor to the synagogue. Some had the shakes. Others made faces or drooled. They mostly didn't speak, and the few that did mumbled, so you couldn't understand them.

Years later Adam thought, what a crazy place for a young boy to get his Jewish education. Why had his parents taken him there? There was a nice Young Israel Reform Temple just a few blocks further away, but his father would say, "It's not Jewish enough; besides, it's a *mitzvah*, a good deed, to worship together with the sick people at the Beth Abraham Home for the Incurables."

Adam put up with it even though he wondered if the Reform Temple was "not Jewish enough," maybe the Beth Abraham Home for the Incurables was too Jewish. And when he learned about the Holocaust, he tended to conflate Beth Abraham with the Nazi horrors.

Adam was thinking about that hospital now, as he sat in his car. He had recently read a book called *Awakenings* by a doctor who had worked in that very hospital. There was talk of a movie someday. The book was about how the doctor brought some of the patients back to life using an experimental drug. But he had to keep giving them higher and higher dosages. Eventually, it was too dangerous to go higher, and the incurables lapsed back into their comatose state.

One of the incurables was a woman—not comatose—who lay on a gurney at the back of the synagogue and held a white plastic object like a shoehorn in her mouth and had what seemed a permanent rubbery smile. Once, just after services ended, she beckoned to Adam, and rather fearfully, he went over to her. "Hey, Sonny," she said. "You want to come to my room?"

"Uh, no thanks," he said. But afterwards he was sorry he hadn't taken her up on it. He was thirteen, and his only sexual experience was playing spin the bottle at parties. He had never come close to being alone with a girl or a woman—even though he thought about them regularly and often drew pictures of naked ones with big breasts, especially during math class. Going to the woman's room had been his chance to possibly have a sexual adventure, and he blew it.

Only, this woman was ugly and crazy, and maybe her terrible disease was contagious. Still, she was likely offering something. He had his chance to be the first with a woman in some fashion before any of his friends. Charlie Taub had made vague claims, but none of the boys believed him. Charlie was always boasting about something that turned out to be untrue.

Maybe he could have seen the woman's breasts, touched them even. It would be years before he would again have such an opportunity. During these years he often fantasized about that woman on the gurney. What exactly would have happened had he gone to her room?

One incurable was different from the others. He was short and very muscular and didn't seem to have anything wrong with his head. He walked around with a small wheelbarrow between his bowed legs, holding the shafts outside his thighs with his huge arm muscles. Everywhere he went he carried his balls in the wheelbarrow, sheathed in extra-large shorts that came down below his knees. It was said that he had the only case of elephantiasis in New York history—had caught it in Africa somewhere.

"That guy has some balls," Adam's friends who were also being tutored by the rabbi for their bar mitzvahs would say. They weren't certain whether to be horrified at, or envious of, the man with the huge balls. They didn't know his name, but they referred to him as "Basketballs." What if having such balls was a good thing? What if girls liked you better if you had such balls just as Adam and the other boys were fascinated by girls' breasts, the bigger the better. Breasts were beautiful, while balls were, well, just balls. And hairy. Also, if your balls were that big and your dick was normal size, it might be a disadvantage. Big balls would make a normal sized dick look smaller, and dicks were more important than balls. Having an enormous dick too—now that would be splendid. But no one said anything about the man having elephantiasis of the dick.

As Adam sat there in his car, he continued thinking about the Beth Abraham Home for the Incurables. Maybe he would write about the place someday. Not like the book he had read—something really freaky and surrealistic. Yes, he said to himself, as he turned to start the Chevy, but his fingers didn't quite reach the keys, and his hand dropped in his lap. His imagination floated more freely than ever.

It was a dark night, and he was walking down a long, lonely street. He spied, blocks ahead, a line of incurables advancing towards him in their white pajamas. As they approached, they pointed fingers at him and chanted something. At first, he couldn't make it out, but as they got closer, he realized what they were saying: "Not Jewish enough, not Jewish enough." It was as if the only way to be sufficiently Jewish was to become one of the incurables.

He turned and ran down the street away from the incurables. But, wait: who was that coming toward him in their black uniforms? He could make out Himmler, Goebbels, Goering, Hess, and, yes, Hitler too. They were prancing along the street, beating whips against their high, shiny boots and chanting something while pointing at Adam. Now, he could hear it. "Too Jewish," they were saying, "too Jewish."

He turned to go the other way, but the incurables were still advancing. There was no way out: he was trapped between the incurables and the Nazis. As both groups closed in on him, he ducked into a door that opened onto the street. Racing up several flights of stairs, he let himself into a vacant apartment on the top floor and made his way to the front windows.

Just below, the incurables and the Nazis were battling. The incurables on gurneys were cutting the Nazis down with their crutches and canes. The incurable with the big balls was swinging his little wheelbarrow with those powerful arms of his. Those in wheelchairs ran over the arms and legs of the Nazis and they screamed. But they also managed to knock down some incurables and beat them with their whips.

The struggle went on and on. The black clad Nazis and the incurables in their white pajamas began to blend into one another until the whole street was awash in a gray tide that slowly ascended the walls of the buildings bordering the street. This terrible mixture was about to reach the window where Adam was watching. He would drown in it. There was no escape...

Adam shivered as he came out of his dreamlike state. He smiled ruefully. Wasn't it enough growing up knowing about the Nazis who wanted to kill him without attending a synagogue full of the strangest Jewish people on the planet? Being a Jew was a perilous business. If the Nazis didn't get you, you might end up an incurable.

Or more likely, you might find yourself sitting in your car, in the middle of a parking lot, staring straight ahead but seeing nothing, hopelessly in love with a woman who was German and a lesbian and who had departed his life forever.

CHAPTER 7

These last thoughts brought Adam fully out of his reverie and back into his misery. Didn't he have enough losing Zoe—however impossible she was for him? Besides, he couldn't sit in his car forever at the Grand Canyon thinking about Nazis and Incurables.

He had to go. But where?

He had originally planned to continue on to California—passing through Las Vegas, Death Valley, Yosemite, and then to the coast and up to San Francisco. Getting as far away from New Jersey and his failed marriage as possible. Radically changing the scene had suited him just fine when he planned the trip. But now? Where could he go to escape his misery over Zoe?

It comforted him to think of traveling north of San Francisco to the giant Redwoods. He had been there as a boy with his parents; if heaven existed, it was in the Redwoods. One could die in the Redwoods with no regrets. Considering how he felt, it wouldn't be an entirely bad idea. Perhaps he could just sink into the rich, dark earth surrounding those trees and become one with them.

He started the car and drove to the parking lot exit, making a point not to look at the canyon. It would be too painful a reminder that Zoe was gone forever. She's German and a lesbian he reminded himself. Forget her. But those days with her had been the most joyful of his life.

He hesitated at the exit. West or east? West had been the plan, but east would put him three thousand miles closer to Zoe, with only an ocean…Stop it he told himself. Thinking this way was madness; he needed to get her off his mind and consider those days with her as a wonderful adventure, nothing more. He turned west, prepared to follow his original itinerary.

It was already dark as he approached Las Vegas, but the lights of the casinos and hotels illuminated the desert for miles. Entering the city, he drove down the twelve-mile strip in wonder at the enormous signs that stood five and six stories high. The tacky glitz of Las Vegas would never gladden his heart under any circumstances, but he felt obliged to experience it. He was a professor and a writer; he should be familiar with such places. He parked and went into one of the casinos. Watching the sad and lonely old men and women with plastic cups filled with quarters feeding them into slot machines made him sadder and lonelier than he already was.

The one tolerable thing about Las Vegas was you could get good bagels, perhaps because it was founded largely by Jewish gangsters. There was a bagel joint just around the corner from the casino where he had stopped. When Adam grew up, bagels were a Jewish thing; you could only get them in Jewish bakeries. When walking with his parents to services at the Beth Abraham Home for the Incurables and wearing a yarmulke, non-Jewish kids would yell, "Hey, where ya goin' bagel-head?" Liking bagels as much as he did, he had never found that offensive, but maybe it was.

Now bagels were becoming ubiquitous in America. No one even thought of them as Jewish anymore. You could get bagels anywhere in America—in Des Moines, Iowa, in Montana, and in Alaska for Chrissake. Shops in the most out of the way places sported names like Bagel Nosh, Bagel-a-Rama, and Bagel Heaven. Zoe had said that there was already a bagel place in Berlin, part of the offerings of a Jewish bakery. Jews had contributed much to world culture, Adam thought, but bagels might just top the list.

He arrived at Yosemite. It was beautiful—the massive El Capitan, the magnificent waterfalls plummeting to the valley floor, but he was too distracted by his troubles to appreciate it. What was the point of Yosemite if he could not experience its natural wonders with Zoe, as he had the Grand Canyon?

He stopped two days in San Francisco, staying in a motel near the Presidio, walked up and down the city's great hills over and over, exhausting himself as if this might diminish his misery over Zoe. Perhaps if he punished himself, actually suffered, he would agonize over Zoe less. Also, vigorous exercise, he knew, was sometimes the best cure for sadness and even depression. Was he depressed or just very sad? He wasn't sure.

In his wanderings through the streets of the city, he came upon a parade. He watched it for a while from the sidewalk and thought there was something very different about it. Then he knew: he saw two men wearing nothing but jockstraps and sneakers who carried a large sign: SIXTH ANNUAL GAY PRIDE PARADE. It was mostly men in the parade, but there were women too. Several of them carrying parasols were topless. Adam wondered what nudity had to do with being gay, but there was comradery among those people which made him feel even lonelier.

Was it possible Zoe would march in such a parade? He couldn't imagine it. But if she did, and he really loved her, lesbian or not, would he march in such a parade with her to show his support? Well, she wasn't here, was she? He didn't have to make that decision.

Back in his car, he crossed the Golden Gate Bridge, planning to head north towards the redwoods. The bridge was scary. There was no barrier between the north and south bound lanes. A head on collision was possible with just one moment of inattention. Adam had to say this for New Jersey: every road of any size was divided by concrete barriers, but then all of New Jersey was concrete.

California was hilly and rugged on the north side of the bridge, but that was only a foretaste of its beauty. Soon he came to the first of the giant redwoods, Muir Woods. He parked and entered their velvety, dark precincts. Even the trees could not compensate for his feelings of loss. Deep among them and alone, with fog rolling in off the sea and soft green moss underfoot, he yelled Zoe's name up into the boughs of a tree that must have been twenty-five feet wide at its base. Perhaps soon, shaken loose by his cries, she would tumble down, limb by limb, into his arms. Or she would come running around from the other side of the tree, shouting to him as she came that she had only been kidding about being a lesbian, perhaps even about being German, that she was going to be with him forever. In the magical Redwoods one could believe anything.

Adam heard footsteps muffled by the forest floor, and then someone was indeed coming towards him from the other side of the tree. Could it be? No, it was a stooped, gray haired man wearing a San Francisco Giants baseball cap, leaning on a cane. "Are you trying to find someone?" he asked. "I heard you calling. Is someone lost?"

Adam was tempted to say someone was indeed lost, lost forever—him, but decided to keep it simple. "No, I'm just shouting something to see if there might be an echo in these trees."

"Is there?" the man asked.

"No," Adam said. "No echo at all."

CHAPTER 8

Making his way out of the grove of giant trees, he located his Chevy in the roadside parking lot. Now he would turn east, though he knew nothing awaited him there except his job and getting ready for fall courses. Driving through the West had not diminished Zoe's presence in his thoughts nor his sadness.

He met people along the road. Thousands of young people were traveling around the country this summer with their thumbs out. Adam picked up whoever needed a ride—men, women, couples. He had regularly hitchhiked when he was younger. There was satisfaction in returning the favor. Sure, there was the possibility of picking up someone crazy—perhaps a serial killer—but in his present mood he hardly cared.

One young couple, probably in their late twenties—the man bearded with dark hair to his shoulders and the woman wearing a long, colorful peasant skirt and pink T-shirt, obviously braless—were hitching their way back to a commune some thirty miles away in southern Utah. Adam wondered what a commune was doing in Utah; these people definitely were not Mormons. When the woman lifted her arms, Adam could see that she didn't shave her armpits. She must have noticed him looking because she said, "We believe in being natural." He noticed her legs were unshaven too. "Why do women have to shave their arm pits and legs if men don't?" she asked. She had a point, but still…Anything that further differentiated the sexes and made women nicer to look at was alright with him.

The couple had some grass with them, which Adam welcomed because he had used up the little he had left the first night with Zoe and he needed a vacation from his sadness. Of course, grass tends to intensify emotions, so there was a danger that things might go the other way—greater grief.

Just short of the commune, his passengers pointed to a dirt road that led down to a creek. They all sat under a tree that hung over the creek, cooling their feet in the water and passing around a joint. Adam had always loved rivers—the mystery of not knowing where they came from, where they were going. Just now the creek was a reminder that he didn't know where he was going. He wished he could be a stick thrown into the water and go wherever the creek would take him.

Loosened up by the grass, Adam talked about his love affair at the Grand Canyon. He didn't mention the German part—the lesbian part was enough. These younger people, like his students, even if they happened to be Jewish, probably wouldn't think about Germans the way he did. The Germans and Nazis would be two different people: the Nazis evil but ancient history, mixed up with other tyrants of the past such as Genghis Khan and Attila the Hun.

For Adam, Germans and Nazis remained the same, except for Zoe. He was fully ready now to make an exception for Zoe, but a thought had begun gnawing at him. If Zoe was so lovely and fine, what about the rest of today's Germans? There were surely other Zoes out there. There was Annika, for instance. If Zoe loved her, how bad could she be? And she, like Zoe, was considering becoming a Jew no less.

"Was I crazy?" Adam asked the young couple. "I fell in love with a lesbian."

"Heavy!" the young man said. "But you didn't know…"

"Well, she said she was. And then for two solid days she was anything but. And then she was again, like a light switch, on and off and on again."

"People are complicated," the young man said. "Freud said we're all bisexual to a lesser or greater degree."

"Maybe so," Adam said, "but I don't feel like I've been missing out on anything being only attracted to women. Anyway, that's what I told her, that she was bisexual, but she insisted otherwise."

The young woman crouched over Adam, hugging him from behind. "*Love is all you need,*" she sang, repeating the refrain from the Beatles song over and over. "*Love is all you need. Love is all you need.*" Then she added, "Doesn't matter what kind." Knowing that Adam was a writer—she had actually read one of his books—she said, "You should write about this. Not in fiction. In life anything's possible. In fiction a lesbian making passionate love to a man and falling in love with him, and him with her, wouldn't be believable—even though it happened. Put it into a memoir. People will believe anything if it's in a memoir. You tell them you've been to the moon and found that it's made of blue cheese, and they'll believe you."

"I'm never going to write about this," Adam said.

"Too personal?"

"Too painful. I thought she was my future."

"What was her name?"

"Zoe."

"I've always liked that name, Zoe."

"Me too. It's Greek for life. I've never known a woman so full of life. Nothing remotely as sexual ever happened to me before, and it happened with someone who insists she's a lesbian."

It was quiet for a while. Adam listened to the water trickle over the stones, making them clank together, a wonderful percussion sound. But without Zoe the music had no melody. He found himself sorry he had spoken about Zoe, as if what had passed between them was so private, sacred even, that it was almost blasphemous to talk about it. Also, talking about it made him feel worse, salt in his wounds—better to tough it out on his own. "Come on," he said. "I'll take you to your commune."

"Maybe you'd like to stay with us a while," the young woman said. "We have room for you in our hut. The commune only charges guests ten dollars a day for food— vegetarian. Everything else would be free. Plenty of pot available—we grow good stuff. We practice free love, by the way."

"Really? I don't mean to pry, but what about you two?"

"Oh," she said, "we're mostly with each other but with other people too when we feel like."

"No jealousy?"

"Jealousy is so yesterday."

"Brother Peter doesn't believe in exclusive attachments," the young man added.

"Who's Brother Peter?"

"An enlightened dude," the young man said. "He founded the commune; he's our leader though we don't call him that. A lot of us were into hard drugs back in Haight-Asbury in San Francisco. Our place would help you get your mind off Zoe, believe me. Some of the women in our place will just love you. You're a professor, a writer, and you're not ugly. You'll have to fight them off."

It was a tempting offer. When they pulled up at the gates of the commune, Adam noticed that, just like his passengers, the men gathered about were bearded with long hair, the women all wore flowery peasant skirts, brightly colored T-shirts and were braless. It's the Seventies, Adam thought. Women are throwing off all restraints.

Some of the women smiled at him and were pretty and appealing. Perhaps he could begin to forget about Zoe here. But he didn't want to forget about Zoe. Not yet. Maybe not ever.

Besides, there was something disconcerting about the fact that all the men and all the women looked the same, as if they were wearing uniforms. And what was with this Brother Peter guy? He probably discouraged exclusive attachments, so everyone would be attached to him. If you fell in love with someone in particular, you'd probably be an outcast in this place. Adam told himself that loneliness, even nursing his pain over Zoe, was better than putting himself into such a situation. Whatever his troubles, he didn't need a cult just now.

His passengers got out of the car. Adam got out for a moment too, and the three hugged before he drove off, looking at all those attractive women in his rearview mirror and wondering whether leaving had been the right choice.

A day later and further east, there was another hitchhiker, a young woman maybe eighteen, maybe twenty-five. She was in torn jeans with her hair in a ponytail. She asked if he would drop her in Denver. "Sure, why not?" he said. He didn't really care where he went as long as it was east, and he was glad for the company. He had several bags of trail mix and some bananas in the car and shared them with her.

Three hundred miles later, the young woman got out of the car next to a phone booth on a downtown Denver street, saying a friend would be picking her up there when she called her. She came around to Adam's side, leaned in the open window, and said, "You're a nice guy. Most other guys who give me a ride want something in return."

"What?"

"Usually a hummer. I don't mind; I mean it isn't sex or anything. But still…" her voice trailed off.

"What's a hummer?" Adam had never heard the term before.

"I read in a book that it's called *fellatio*. Sounds like someone in Shakespeare that we studied in school."

"That's Horatio. He's in *Hamlet*."

"Whatever...Most people call it a blow job, but I don't like that word, especially the *job* part.

What the young woman said about the "job" part of the word blow job reminded Adam of his sexual relationship with his wife. That had been a job. With Zoe everything had just happened—naturally, smoothly, absent all effort.

"It's like in restaurants," the young woman went on, "where the waiter asks you, 'You still workin' on that?' You're paying good money and enjoying yourself, and the waiter wants to know if you're still *working*. That's why I say hummer. It's more casual."

Adam had to agree, but his adolescence had been in the Fifties, before, as he often joked, oral sex had been invented. Sex had been described in baseball terminology: first base—a kiss; second base—touching a breast or, even better, both; third base—some below the waist activity; and a home run—sexual intercourse. A blow job, which he had heard of back then but not experienced, seemed so erotic he would have thought of it as a grand slam, a home run with the bases loaded. But now, according to this young woman, it had become an everyday form of activity. It wasn't even sex.

She went on to tell of a man who had offered her a ride and wanted to kiss her "before I gave him the hummer. He was older, like you. I told him no. I had to draw the line somewhere."

Adam was intrigued by these new sexual mores. Kissing, the new second base, above blow jobs on the intimacy scale. Kissing was serious, important, an expression of love. A blow job was just a friendly act.

She paused and turned to watch someone enter the phone booth. "You're not gay, are you? I mean I could still come back in the car and…"

"No," he said, "you're very nice, but my mind is totally on another woman just now."

"You're in love," she said.

He nodded.

"That's beautiful," she said. "Everybody should be in love."

Yes, Adam thought to himself. But maybe not with a German lesbian he would never see again.

The young woman put her head through the window and kissed him on the cheek. "You're sweet," she said. "You, I want to kiss."

He smiled and patted her cheek. He could see that the phone booth was vacant again, so he pointed to it and drove off. He felt good that the young woman considered him sweet and that he had sought no compensation for the ride. Better to give than to receive and all that. When he was in his teens, sex was not something you shared but tried to get—and half of it was being able to brag to your friends, to be the first to get to one of those bases. It was like scaling a mountain or catching a touchdown pass.

Now one-way sex had no appeal to Adam; it wasn't, well, sexy—hadn't been for a long time. He thought of it as clinical, something administered by medical personnel. No wonder so many men had fantasies about having sex with nurses.

Besides, as with the women at the commune, sex with anyone just now would, he thought, cheapen all that happened at the Grand Canyon. He didn't want this. He was keeping alive a lost cause, but it was his cause. Still, he couldn't help asking himself, what am I, some kind of monk? He decided things might go easier if he didn't pick up any more female hitchhikers.

One day he drove nineteen hours and seven hundred thirty-six miles. He wasn't sure what the hurry was in getting back to New Jersey, but he just kept going—taking some satisfaction in his endurance, at the number of miles he could achieve in one day, as if he had something to prove. He realized that he was punishing himself again, the way he had on the hills of San Francisco—suffering to diminish the larger ache.

In southern Indiana, exhausted, he pulled off the interstate and entered a dull, gray town whose key feature was a grain elevator. The town's all but abandoned Main Street included a closed movie house whose marquee announced the Reverend Smiley Brothers' next sermon: "JESUS LOVES RICH PEOPLE." You could always tell a town was on the skids when the evangelists took over the movie houses and preached about how Jesus was the first capitalist. If you believed in Jesus, you got rich.

Past a boarded-up store front was the Imperial Hotel. It was unclear whether the hotel was operating because he was able to park directly in front of it—no meters, no signs. But the door swung open when he pushed on it. In the dimly lit lobby, the carpeting was so threadbare the wood flooring showed through in spots. An old, white-haired man, a permanent guest Adam surmised, snored in an armchair, and a man not much younger stood blinking behind the front desk. A large clock on the wall above him was hours off or had stopped long ago. It was as if he had stumbled into the 1930s or an episode of that old television drama, *The Twilight Zone*. The place creeped him out. If he hadn't been exhausted, he would have gotten back on the road and sought lodging elsewhere.

As he signed the register, Adam was alerted by the desk clerk that the television set in his room, a black and white with rabbit ears as it turned out, might not be working. He didn't care; all he needed was a bed. After being handed a large skeleton key attached to a chain—plastic card keys had yet to arrive at the Imperial—he found his room on the dimly lit third floor.

He hung a partially torn DO NOT DISTURB sign on the outside doorknob and tried to pull down the shades on the windows, but they kept snapping up again. Finally, he managed to tie one to the radiator by its pull string, but the other was hopeless—it would have to remain up. There was a dingy chenille bedspread on the bed with brown crumbs of some sort between its ridges—or were they bits of rust from a plumbing leak in the room above? There were large brown stains on the ceiling. The stains and the crumbs hardly mattered. He barely got his clothes off before tumbling onto the narrow bed and falling asleep.

CHAPTER 9

Awakening in a great sweat, Adam looked at his watch. He had slept eleven hours, and the entire time, or so it seemed, he had a strange dream. Or was it a dream? It wasn't about Zoe, but about his wife or someone who resembled her. Perhaps his unhappiness with Zoe had catapulted him back into preoccupations over his defunct marriage. He lay there trying to recall the dream before he forgot it, slowly sorting out what was his dream and what was his real life.

The wife in his dream had a mustache. It wasn't so much the indignity of being married to a woman with a mustache—though he imagined people whispering behind his back: "See that guy? He's married to the woman with the mustache; poor schmuck can't do better than a woman with a mustache." But it was the kind of mustache, more than its presence, that was especially troubling. It was coarse, dark, narrow. It seemed to hang beneath her nose rather than ride her lip. It looked like Hitler's mustache up there under her nose.

There were times in recent months when his real wife's attitude towards him had made him think Hitler hadn't died in that Berlin bunker, that he was living in a center hall colonial in East Mount View, New Jersey, only one mile from the Miracle Mall. Zoe said he was married to Hitler. She'd meant it in another way—his obsession. Given the woman in his dream, he might, until his divorce came through, indeed be married to Hitler.

Okay, he was exaggerating. But was it a mere coincidence that his wife was born on April 30, 1945, the very day of Hitler's suicide? Hitler's untranquil spirit could have entered her mother's womb early that day thinking, "This is a perfect hideout. They'll never suspect a little Jewess." Had Hitler's spirit lain dormant in his wife since birth, emerging to begin its new depredations on the world, warming up to the task by torturing her husband? Like Hitler, his wife was short and angry. And if her recent treatment of him was any indication, Hitler hadn't the slightest remorse for the Holocaust and World War II. He only wished he could have done more. Next time: No more Mr. Nice Guy.

Images of the Holocaust and Hitler had crowded into Adam's dream. All six million were there, with tattooed numbers not on their arms but on their faces. The tattooed faces made him wonder whether his continuing obsession with Hitler and the Holocaust was an addiction, a secret vice, or even a perversion.

Now there were torchlit Nazi rallies, naked people running past Mengele at Auschwitz, stick-like bodies being fed into ovens, Jews hung from lampposts, Jews shot and pushed into pits they had been forced to dig, Jews choking on the green gas emerging from shower heads.

His half wakeful mind, jumping from subject to subject, still wanted to know whether there was a mustache under his wife's nose in his dream. Perhaps it was just a mysterious shadow he hadn't noticed before. In bed, he could have reached over her shoulder while she was sleeping and felt around under her nose to see if there was stiff hair there. Or while having sex, he could have pretended to an excess of passion, extending a French kiss beyond her upper lip to see what he encountered. She wouldn't have suspected anything because she considered him a sloppy kisser anyway. "Quit drooling on me," she would say. "If you want to kiss, kiss; stop this drooling business."

But their relationship had deteriorated to the point where he slept in the attic and never got physically close to her. If she was taller, he could have looked at her face-to-face and determined if she had a mustache, and it would have helped if he still had his glasses. He had crushed them underfoot getting out of bed in the attic to descend to the bathroom. But had he really? At the moment, he wasn't sure.

His wife really gave him a start when a lock of her straight black hair fell over her forehead. With the mustache and her limp wristed gestures, she looked like Hitler for sure. Or like a Hitler drag queen—parading around in bra, panties and a garter belt, accessorized with a little whip.

He knew Hitler drove the women in his life crazy just as his wife, more so in the dream, drove him crazy. Hitler's women killed themselves. After meeting him, they either threw themselves into the Rhine or blew their brains out, and not just Eva Braun: seven of the eight women in his life killed themselves, and the sole survivor some suspect was actually a man—biologically anyway.

There was, of course, also Hitler's undescended testicle. One ball up and one ball down doesn't send a very clear message. Nor does parading about as the macho man of the universe when what you really crave is to get buggered by the entire German army.

His dream wife once tried to do it to Adam. She purchased a dildo, strapped it on, and prepared to stick it up his ass—without any foreplay. When he declined, she said, "You fuck me. Why can't I ever fuck you?"

"Don't you think this is carrying feminism a bit far?" he replied, edging away from her. You have your biology and I have mine. There's the fucker and the fuckee."

"Oh," she whined, "you never want to try anything new. Wait till the women in my group hear about this."

Perhaps it was Hitler never wanting to try anything sexual at all that drove Eva Braun to join him in suicide in the bunker? A heterosexual woman might consider suicide if she knew she would never, ever get laid because the guy she was stuck with (assuming she didn't want to be slow hung with piano wire in a meat locker) preferred the company of young men in tight uniforms. Every night Hitler would come home from inspecting the flower of Aryan manhood and did he want to fool around? He'd give Eva a peck on the cheek—especially when she wore jodhpurs and leggings—but mostly, he kept her around for appearance sake and to secretly borrow her lingerie. With Eva he played patty-cake or, given his obsession with excrement, got her to shit on him once in a while. She wasn't too keen on it. Urinating on him was tolerable, but shitting?

While Eva felt there was something missing in her relationship with Hitler, the prestige of being the Führer's girl had its compensations. And she did admire him. "Ach, Ady," she would say, "he's too good; he's a saint." Of course, if Ady had been a little less of a saint—maybe gotten laid once in a while, whether by man, woman, or beast, millions of lives might have been saved.

Adam's wife certainly hadn't gotten laid much lately, at least not by him, especially since she proposed using the dildo on him. Now there was the mustache. Might the lack of sex have brought on this Hitler mustache thing, some hormonal imbalance?

Maybe his mother had some idea about his wife's mustache. In his dream he visited her at her condo in Florida. They sat out on her balcony watching the sunset on the water, while he asked for her advice.

"Do you think there's something strange about her?"

"Strange?" his mother replied.

"Lately she looks like Hitler to me."

"Well," his mother said, "Didn't I and your father, may he rest in peace, warn you about marrying shiksas?" To Adam's mother, any woman with a nose smaller than Barbra Streisand's had to be a shiksa.

"She's not a shiksa," Adam said. He mentioned famous Jews with no more nose than a couple of holes in their faces. He mentioned celebrity converts to Judaism. "What about Elizabeth Taylor and Marilyn Monroe?"

"Good for them that they converted," his mother replied. "I've never been able to understand worshipping that *meshugana* Jew, Jesus."

"Sammy Davis, Jr. is another one who converted to Judaism."

"Oy, Sammy Davis," his mother said. "Doesn't he have trouble enough being a one-eyed, dancing schwartze without being Jewish too?"

And then in the dream, he was asleep back in the attic. Footsteps were slowly mounting the stairs. Was it his wife? Hitler? Both? There he was, as helpless as Anne Frank in the secret annex, and the number one Nazi was coming to get him. She held a mask with a rubber hose connected to a tank of Zyklon B. She leaned over him, her mustache twitching and gleaming in the dark. The mask was descending…

That must have woken him because he remembered getting up to pee. His sheets were soaked with sweat—no air conditioning in the Imperial Hotel. "Phew," he said out loud, "what a dream. Enough of that." Falling onto the bed again, he was instantly back in the dream. At least it was what he remembered the next morning as he lay there sorting out what was the dream and what was his life.

His wife was calling him down from the attic to explain a thick scum of shaving cream and whiskers hanging off the edge of the bathroom sink. "You should talk about whiskers," he considered saying. Instead, as she stood there with her arms crossed, waiting for him to do something about the sink, he clicked his heels together, stuck his right arm stiffly out in front of him, and yelled, "Jawohl mein Führer."

"Very funny," she said.

He noticed his wife drinking her morning coffee out of the porcelain mustache cup. She had never used it before; it was a knickknack with a sunset painted on it that sat on the shelf in the split pediment dining room cabinet. It was just for show. Whenever she said "for show," he cringed. "A real conversation piece" was another saying of hers that constituted fingernails scraping on his personal blackboard. When they had people over for dinner, she delighted in getting down the mustache cup and explaining how it kept a man's mustache out of his tea or coffee, the mustache resting on the shelf across the rim of the cup with the little opening through which the liquid was sipped.

Now she was drinking from the mustache cup. Was this proof the mustache on her face was real?

"How come you're drinking coffee from the mustache cup?" he wanted to know.

She was furious. "You always complained because I didn't use the cabinet things," she shouted. "Now you complain because I am using them?" He retreated to his lair in the attic.

The next morning, there she was again, drinking her coffee out of the mustache cup. That night, he stole downstairs from the attic to the kitchen, opened the dishwasher, and examined the mustache cup. He handled it gingerly, hoping it would offer some clue—a telltale hair at the bottom of the cup or some mustache shaped imprint on the mustache protector. As he examined the cup, turning it from side to side and holding it up to the light, it slipped from his grasp; as he watched in horror, it plummeted to the ceramic tile floor and broke into pieces.

What to do? There was an old tube of glue in his tool chest in the basement. Hopefully, it wasn't dried out. Maybe he could glue the pieces together and his wife would never know the difference.

No, she would have to be blind not to notice, and it would surely leak. He had to get rid of the cup. Hopefully, she would think she had misplaced it, would search days before giving up. How could he get rid of the smashed cup? If he put the pieces into the garbage can, she would see them.

He put a windbreaker on over his pajamas, got the spade out of the garage, and began digging a hole under the red maple at the back of the garden. The digging went slowly because he kept hitting roots. He could only scratch a hole two inches deep. To cover some of the larger pieces he had to crush them with the spade.

The noise must have awakened his wife. He heard a window open. Looking up at the house, he saw her small head framed in the bedroom window. Her long, five-battery flashlight was trained on him. He felt like a concentration camp prisoner trapped in the beam of a watchtower searchlight. He could hear dogs barking somewhere in the night. "What are you doing out there?" she demanded.

Thinking fast, he said, "Digging for worms."

"What for? You hate fishing."

"I thought I might go on Saturday," he rejoined.

She closed the window.

He prayed that was the end of it, but when he came down for breakfast the next day, the pieces of mustache cup, covered with dirt, sat on the drain board by the kitchen sink. His wife had gotten up early and exhumed them from their shallow grave. She stood beside them now, her arms crossed over her chest, her eyes blazing. "Would you mind telling me why you went outside in the middle of the night, smashed this cup, and buried it?

"That's not exactly how it happened."

"Okay, how did it happen?"

"I was looking at it here in the kitchen and it fell."

"At three in the morning, you were looking at it?"

"That's right."

"Why?"

Why indeed? He looked carefully at her. Was the mustache there or not? Under the cold, fluorescent lights of the kitchen he wasn't sure. The dark shadow was there, but was it hair? "I've…become interested in ceramics," he finally said.

"Let me get this straight," she responded. "Because of this sudden passion for ceramics, you came down to the kitchen from the attic and started rousting about in the dishwasher?"

"Well, yes."

"And then the mustache cup breaks, and you decide to bury it in the backyard?"

"Correct."

"Why didn't you just put it into the garbage? Why this elaborate drama in the middle of the night?"

"I didn't want to hurt your feelings. You've been very attached to that cup lately."

"Yes, I have, haven't I?" How exactly did she mean that? he wondered.

The next evening, he noticed something different about the cabinet: five new mustache cups were behind the glass door, each larger than the original.

There was a step behind him. "I decided to treat myself," his wife said, raising yet another mustache cup full of tea to her lips. This one was considerably larger than the broken one, big enough to hold several servings of chicken noodle soup. It not only covered where her mustache might be; it covered the better part of her face. Her eyes peered out over the top.

He was startled by its immense size. "That sure is an outstanding mustache cup," he said agreeably as possible. "Maybe you could collect one from every country."

Extending this olive branch did little good because later that evening there was a terrible scene. His wife came upon him in the kitchen as he was examining the mammoth mustache cup she had been drinking from earlier. He put it down quickly, but with a maniacal gleam in her eye, she rushed to his study and hoisted his Smith Corona portable typewriter over her head. "See how you feel having something of yours broken," she screamed, and threw the typewriter.

It didn't quite reach the floor. He had raced after her, and just as he entered his study, the typewriter on which he had written his books, the books that had gotten him tenure at the university and some scholarly recognition, crashed down on his right foot. For a moment he felt nothing; then the pain reached his brain, and his brain sent the message back to his foot. He screamed, "Aeeeeeeeeh!" and began hopping about the house in agony.

Later, when he peeled off his shoe, he discovered that his second toe was black. The emergency room at the local hospital took X-rays and confirmed that the toe was broken in two places. Rather than splinting it, they taped it to his big toe, told him not to wear a shoe on that foot for two weeks, and loaned him crutches. Didn't he have enough problems without a smashed toe and crutches? He might have tried to overlook the broken toe and his now incapacitated Smith Corona with the bent return arm and the case so dented it rested on the keys when he attempted to close it—if it hadn't been for the mustache business.

His wife tried to be conciliatory. "I'm sorry about your typewriter and your toe," she said, "but you broke my mustache cup."

That was just like her. She had an equation in her head: intentionally breaking his cherished typewriter and his toe equaled accidentally breaking her mustache cup. To put it another way: what was hers was hers, and what was his was negotiable. The only way to deal with such people was to get them before they got you. You couldn't appease her any more than Hitler. You gave them an inch; they took a country.

He had been socialized never to hit women, whatever the provocation. They were smaller, weaker and, allegedly, meeker. Hitler was small and weak (what was all this Aryan Superman shit?) and, when it came right down to it, meek as well. Ah the meek. Jesus had it wrong. If the meek ever did inherit the earth, it would be curtains for the rest of us.

Some days later, he finally did hit her. She had brought home a dog—a bitch, naturally, and a German Shepherd to boot. Visions of Nazis and their dogs in the death camps smoked in his brain. Now he was racing for the high fence surrounding the camp. He almost made it, but his wife's dog leaped and pulled him down by his frayed cuff. Then it tore out his throat. Nevertheless, he miraculously recovered and was back in New Jersey.

But the dog returned too. It was chasing him around the backyard. Could he get over that fence? Suddenly a gate in the fence opened and Zoe beckoned to him. "This way," she said. He went through the gate; it closed behind him, but she wasn't there.

His wife called her dog Poupée. She said it was French for doll. He thought *schweinhund* would have been more appropriate. From the moment Poop arrived on the scene there was bad blood between them, as there had been between him and an earlier dog of his wife's, a dachshund. What was it with her and these Kraut dogs? He thought it was only a matter of time before Poop attacked him. And he suspected just where she would attack him. Whenever Poop was near, he kept his hands clasped in front of his crotch.

"Why does your dog hate me so much?" he asked his wife when she had just come in from walking Poop.

"She's just being friendly," she replied—which is what dog owners always say when their beasts slaver all over your best pants, fresh from the cleaners, or when you frantically point to your infant daughter's head wedged in their jaws.

"Friendly?! Like what, a rabid wolf? I don't see why I should have to put up with her abuse in my own home."

"Her abuse?" his wife sneered, her mustache more apparent than ever. It was quivering there beneath her nose.

Later that evening he went up to his attic room and there, in the middle of the oval hooked rug, was a steaming pile of fresh dog shit. Was this Poop just being friendly?

He yelled down the stairs to his wife, but she didn't answer. He hobbled down the two flights on his crutches and confronted her in the kitchen. "Your dog," he said, "has shat on my rug."

"So?"

"So, I want it cleaned up."

"Clean it up yourself," she said, returning to the book she was reading, William Shirer's *The Rise and Fall of the Third Reich*. He wondered which she favored, the rise or the fall?

"It's...your dog," he sputtered in rage

"It's your room," she responded. "I'm not your maid," she said rising to confront him.

This was too much. "Clean up what your fucking dog has done in my room," he shouted.

"Don't you dare use filthy language around Poupée," she quietly hissed between clenched teeth, as if Poop was an impressionable young child who needed to be spared any vulgarity. She dug her nails into his arm as she said this.

It hurt but he was close enough to her now that he was sure the mustache was there—black and glistening with evil. With that wild look in her eyes, his wife had never resembled Hitler more.

The combination of her mustache, his broken toe, and the pain in his arm was too much. "Nazi bitch," he screamed, slapping her across the cheek with his free hand in an attempt to get her to release his arm. It was a light slap, but his fingertips caught the edge of her nose and there was a snapping sound.

Just his luck: the one time he slaps her in eight years of marriage, while regularly absorbing physical abuse from her—she had probably slapped him a dozen times—and he breaks her nose. If she'd had a strong, decent sized Jewish nose instead of that little snout of hers, it wouldn't have happened. She went to the emergency room at the hospital and returned with a white mask on her face made of plaster impregnated gauze. It proved to be a big hit at her women's group, a graphic example of men's brutality. She got all the women to sign it with ballpoint pens. One of them wrote, "Fuck men!" above her signature. Adam assumed this was not meant in a sexually inviting way. Or was this sentiment what inspired his wife to try the dildo on him?

Within two weeks, each of them had dispatched the other to the emergency room at the hospital. Unlike him, however, his wife had no compunctions about getting a lawyer and filing a complaint. The next day he was issued a court order barring him from living in his own home. Had he been given the opportunity to defend himself, he would have told the judge that he had hit his wife in self-defense. He would have shown the judge his broken toe and the fresh scars on his arm.

But he was happy to go. He relished never having to mow his lawn again—and it was bigger than most because the house was on a cul-de-sac. A cul-de-sac: that seemed to sum up his and his wife's relationship. Almost as appropriate as a dead end.

His wife's birthday was coming up in a few days. Now he wouldn't have to ponder what to get her. He had also been concerned that, in celebrating in some fashion, they might have had more than a little to drink, waxed nostalgically, and given their moribund sex life the old college try.

Admittedly, his penis had functioned adequately in other challenging circumstances. But with a woman who now looked like Adolf Hitler? He wasn't sure which would be more humiliating: not being able to get it up or getting it up. Probably the latter. One could carry perversity only so far.

Finally, there was an overriding reason to leave the house on Deerpath Road: his wife's upcoming birthday would be her thirtieth and the thirtieth anniversary of Hitler's suicide. Who knew what Pandora's box of horrors might be opened by this combination of events: the moon turning blood red, wolves howling, toilets overflowing, the Four Horsemen of the Apocalypse laying waste to the Jersey suburbs? He might need to run for his life from his wife and her minions. Better to leave now.

Also, if he stayed longer in that house there would be blood on the walls. He or his wife would be dead and the other in jail forever. The court order had decided for him what he hadn't been quite capable of deciding for himself—to begin a new life.

And with that, Adam stopped thinking about his dream and fully segued into the present. He got out of the bed in his crummy room in the Imperial Hotel and took a shower in the slim trickle that emerged from the shower head, just enough to wash off the sweat. By now he knew most of what he had dreamed had never happened, but he was reluctant to let go of it. Why had his wife inhabited the dream? Wasn't he through with her, or was she still following him, she and Hitler. Maybe Zoe was only half right. It wasn't just an obsession. He was actually married to Hitler.

He was worn out by his long dream. He put on his glasses, which hadn't been stepped on and broken as in the dream. He wondered whether dreaming of broken glasses had some dark symbolic meaning. Perhaps a personal Kristallnacht, the November 1938 night of the Broken Glass when the Nazis smashed the windows of Jewish shopkeepers throughout Germany, attacked Jews in the street, and burned synagogues.

He checked out of the hotel. He found the only restaurant in town where he could get breakfast—just down the street from the closed movie theatre where the Reverend Smiley Brothers would soon be speaking.

Sure enough: even here in this nearly dead Indiana town, bagels were on the menu. Frozen ones—plain, no everything bagels, no seeds at all—so he ordered bacon and eggs. Drinking the poisonous coffee as he waited for his food, he wondered why he hadn't imagined Zoe instead of his wife with a Hitler mustache? No, he decided. While his experience with Zoe may have inspired his dream, when it came to evoking Hitler, Zoe, German and all, couldn't compete with his wife.

CHAPTER 10

It was Labor Day weekend, and Adam hadn't been in his New Jersey apartment for an entire day before he broke down and phoned Zoe. He hadn't entirely given up hope—anything was possible. Perhaps when she returned home to Annika, Zoe discovered she preferred him! Or at the very least, now realized she was bisexual. Perhaps she was questioning her life and now craved being with him—or even just partially with him; he could settle for that. Maybe she was as mistaken about her sexuality as he was—or had been—about today's Germans.

Getting through was difficult. He had no phone or address for her, and according to the operator, there were two women in West Berlin with her first and last names. There also was the seven-hour time difference to be reckoned with. He decided to call both numbers. Luckily, he reached Zoe with the first.

"Hallo," she said. Adam wondered if that's how you said hello in Germany or if it was her accent. No doubt her accent was more pronounced to his ear than when he was with her. Then all his senses had been tuned to her frequency and her slight accent of little consequence.

"Zoe, this is Adam."

Silence on the other end. At least she wasn't hanging up. Finally, she said, "Did you see my message on the mirror?"

"Yes," Adam said, "and I shouldn't have called."

"I meant the rest of the message. I love you, Adam. But…"

"I know. I just needed to hear your voice. I needed to know that everything at the Grand Canyon really happened."

Silence again. "I told Annika about us after all."

"And?"

"She was very hurt and angry. She went out and picked up the first man in the street and went to bed with him."

"I'm sorry," he said.

"No need to be. It was something she needed to do. Things are much better now; we've forgiven each other. And she had more to forgive. After all, I love you; she just wanted to punish me.

"And, Adam," she continued, "Annika and I are taking instruction from a rabbi. We have decided to become Jews. And we hope to have a child, maybe two, and raise them Jewish. Isn't that wonderful?"

"Yes," Adam said. "After the Holocaust, Germany can use some Jews." Like converts to anything, Zoe and her friend (this was the only way he was able to think of Annika, as Zoe's "friend") would end up being better Jews than him.

But a rabbi in Berlin? If a rabbi could tolerate being there…Adam didn't want to finish the sentence, even in his mind.

"Adam, I must go now. I expect Annika home any minute. If she knew I was talking with you, it would make things difficult."

"I understand. I hope you're not angry I called. I couldn't help it. I love you very much."

"I feel the same about you, Adam. You know I do. Just hearing your voice puts me back with you at the Grand Canyon, but I can only lead one life." She was crying now. "I can't bring myself to hang up," she gasped. "Your voice is precious to me. If you love me, you will do me the great favor of hanging up first. I cannot bear to hang up on you."

"Okay," he said, "just so you know: there isn't anything I wouldn't do for you. Anything! Ever! If you need me, just call this number—and he gave her his phone number." With that, he slowly lowered the phone. That night he met a friend and got very, very drunk. That was it—no Zoe.

Then who? And what? What kind of new life was possible in the Walt Whitman apartments? Adam had lived there for a time when he was single, so there was no novelty to the place. Bad as it was then, it had deteriorated somewhat since. The only garden that came with his garden apartment was a patch of mostly dead grass.

Beyond the grass, the brick two-story garden apartment buildings stretched as far as one could see. They looked like barracks, as if the Walt Whitman was a military base. There were occasional, uninspired plantings, but no store, no café, no newsstand, no mailbox, no sidewalks, no porches, not even a bench where people might hang out. You never saw anyone on the paved paths of the development; everyone came and went by automobile. One of the few signs of activity in Walt Whitman was the smell of barbecuing beef and people on their tiny balconies forever grilling.

Nearby, Highway 19 traffic charged by en route to the mall, and Adam's windows rattled continuously. A dusting of dried putty fell like dandruff from the mullions onto the windowsills.

Adam's apartment was so empty every noise sounded hollow. Virtually his sole possession was a queen-sized mattress purchased from Mattress Mode and delivered the day he left on his trip West. It lay on the floor, just as he had left it, all but filling the bedroom of his one-bedroom efficiency. It was still covered in grimy plastic with the C.O.D. tickets taped to it.

And in the tiny living room, he had his desk, a chair, a lamp, and stacks of books on the floor. In the kitchen, he had one pot, some plates, and only enough silverware for himself. This was all his wife let him keep. If he had someone over, they'd have to share the spoon or fork.

The Walt Whitman wasn't entirely different from the village of East Mount View in its absence of civilization, although being within walking distance to campus was a benefit.

Otherwise, Adam's conversation with the downstairs tenant when he moved in—the only conversation they would have—typified the place. As Adam was carrying his desk up the stairs, this neighbor came out of his apartment. He was a hulking giant and wore an old-fashioned sleeveless undershirt, the kind now being called a wife-beater. Hair poked out everywhere. Adam had never seen a hairier man. In their brief conversation, while Adam treacherously balanced two of the desk legs on a stair in front of him, the man, who didn't offer to help with the desk, opined that the garden apartments were named for some rich developer, Mr. Walt Whitman.

"Same name as the poet?" Adam grunted. "Imagine that."

"Huh?" the man said.

When Adam lived there a decade before, the Walt Whitman had been convenient for a young, single professor. It was the perfect place to bring women, as anonymous as a motel. Luckily, this was before sexual harassment became a university obsession. Back then, you almost had to expose yourself in the classroom to be charged with misconduct.

For men, sex had been one of the great things about the feminist revolution. Women embracing sexual freedom meant they were just as ready for anything as men. Men no longer had to wear themselves out pursuing women while fearing rejection. Women often made the first move and called the man on the phone. Also, sex wasn't something you led up to; it was what you started with. If the sex worked out, then you dated—movies, dinner, candlelight, romance, marriage. But first sex. And in most cases only sex.

Most women were on the pill, so you didn't worry about contraception. Men could say, "To hell with condoms." When you used condoms, you weren't inside a woman; it was as if you were inside a plastic bag. Also, you didn't give a thought to venereal disease. Adam had never heard of herpes, and gonorrhea and syphilis could almost always be eliminated by a shot or two in the behind. AIDs had yet to appear.

After Zoe, he now had little interest in other women. When Labor Day weekend came to an end, he taught his classes at the university and brooded over her. He wasn't celibate, but while his penis might be into it, his heart wasn't. His occasional adventures did little to get Zoe out of his mind or lighten his mood. Being in love was like an addiction to a powerful drug. If he couldn't have Zoe, he would have to find someone her equal. Did such a woman exist? One who wasn't a lesbian? Meanwhile, he felt half alive.

CHAPTER 11

His spirits were buoyed a bit when a State Department invitation arrived for him to lecture in India during the winter break. It was always nice to be wanted. His recent book of nonfiction stories focused on the non-assimilative practices of the growing South Asian Indian population in New Jersey. Torn between America and the old ways, most still believed in arranged marriages and consulted astrologists before making major decisions. And Gandhi or not, when it came to marriage, the caste system for them was very much alive.

Adam had never been to India and would be traveling on the U.S. government's dime. With the help of the university's travel agent, he began looking into flights. "Direct or stopover?" the agent asked.

"Direct...I think. Why would I stopover?"

"You have the time and the money. Why not stop in another city en route—Rome, Istanbul, Berlin."

"Definitely not Berlin," he said.

Later, he thought otherwise. Zoe was in Berlin. If he could see her even briefly, just see her and talk, he would break his vow never to even change planes in Germany. Still, why not just remember Zoe at the Grand Canyon?

Why not just remember all that loving instead of being forcefully reminded that she was a German lesbian? He was starving for Zoe—though afraid seeing her might magnify his sorrow.

He was willing to take that chance. If he saw her in the airport, he might technically but not emotionally set foot in Germany. Airport terminals have a neutral quality. There would be nothing particularly German about the terminal; it could be anywhere.

But would Zoe see him? Would she be angry if he called again?

He phoned and told her he might be passing through Berlin airport overnight en route to India. Could he see her?

"So glad you called," she said. "I want to see you too." That was a happy surprise. She couldn't talk just then but would call him back the next day. He sensed she wanted to check with Annika about something.

When she called back, she questioned him. "Meet you in the airport? Why? I know a wonderful Indian restaurant in town."

"I'll have more than enough Indian food in India," Adam replied.

"Besides," Zoe insisted, "Annika and I have plenty of room. You can stay with us over night. Annika wants to meet you. She knows I care about you, and it's okay with her now. If it had been another woman, it might have been different.

"Our relationship is totally healed now, maybe even stronger," she continued. "You're important to Annika because you're important to me. Besides, Annika and I have something we want to discuss with you."

Adam didn't like that *we*. Nor was he keen on meeting Annika—he preferred pretending she didn't exist. What was this *something* they wanted to discuss with him?

"In the airport," he insisted. "It's all I can handle right now. And just you." If he and Zoe were alone, some of the intimacy of the Grand Canyon might be rekindled, even if it wasn't physical, just emotional. That wouldn't happen with Annika present. If Annika were present, he could not indulge his fantasies about Zoe—which included maybe, just maybe, her contemplating a future with him.

Even though he wasn't going beyond the airport, Adam began to read everything he could on post-war Germany, especially Berlin. He told himself it might help him better understand Zoe or maybe she would appreciate his showing some interest in her Germany, the "good" Germany she insisted was real. He studied a little common phrase book, learned such words as *danke* (thank you) and *nein* (no). He rented documentaries about contemporary Germany, feature films too. For the first time he avoided films on the Holocaust which, before, had been the only aspect of Germany he paid attention to, the only aspect that was relevant.

He studied the geography of Berlin, finding himself especially interested in the wall. He had always thought it was short and straight, separating East from West Berlin, but it seemed to actually encircle all of West Berlin for a hundred and two miles. West Berlin was an island surrounded by East Germany. The Communists weren't just concerned about East Berliners escaping into West Berlin; they were also concerned about escapees from anywhere in East Germany.

Adam went back to the travel agent and asked her to make a reservation for one night in a Berlin airport hotel. "The hotel has to be in the airport," he said. "If possible, connected to it." The travel agent found a hotel that connected directly with the terminal, an American hotel. Adam was pleased. He would feel less compromised staying in an American hotel.

"Let's talk airlines now" the travel agent said. Lufthansa would be best. Overnight to Berlin and on to Delhi, India the day after."

"Not Lufthansa." If he didn't drive German cars, he damn well wouldn't fly German airlines Also, Lufthansa sounded too much like Luftwaffe. Lufthansa planes probably had censors in the restrooms to detect Jews. You sat down, a buzzer sounded, and you got sucked out of the plane ass first.

"It's the most convenient to Berlin and moderately priced."

"Any other airline. Not Lufthansa."

CHAPTER 12

At Kennedy Airport, Adam boarded the overnight Pan American flight. He made his way to the window seat he had requested. A window seat gave him some sense of control—that his safety wasn't entirely up to unseen pilots in the front of the plane. If a flight was bumpy, he could look out the window and see the clouds causing the bumpiness and make sure the plane, or at least the wing and motor on his side, was intact. He was also pleased there were only two seats on each side of the plane, so he would have only one fellow passenger to contend with, hopefully not a German.

A couple in their sixties approached, parting at Adam's row. The woman took the aisle seat next to Adam; her husband continued on. Adam soon discovered that she was Danish and spoke excellent English. Ah, the Danes, the good Europeans who saved ninety-five percent of their Jews from the Nazis, hiding them and ferrying them one by one across to neutral Sweden. Their king rode daily on horseback about the streets of Copenhagen and was rumored to wear the yellow Star of David on his arm.

Once the plane had reached cruising altitude, and the captain had turned off the "Fasten Seat belts" sign, the woman kept turning and gesturing to her husband, who was several rows back. Finally, she asked Adam if he would mind having someone else in her seat so she could join her husband. "It will be my pleasure," he told her. Anything for the heroic Danes.

She spoke to the stewardess, who nodded, went back to the husband's row, and spoke to someone who seemed to be in agreement. The Danish woman, thanking Adam, got up and moved up the aisle.

Moments later, an enormously fat, red faced man tumbled into the seat next to Adam. This man was so huge, part of him hung over into the aisle, and he occupied all of the arm rest between himself and Adam and then some. His arms were fatter than Adam's legs. Each time someone came up the aisle, he leaned away from them and onto Adam.

When dinner arrived, Adam was forced to eat with his arms straight out, both elbows tucked into his body. He dropped a dollop of mashed potatoes with gravy onto his lap, most of which he managed with difficulty to extract with his plastic spoon. He used his napkin for the rest, but he was left with a sizeable stain across his crotch.

Soon the cabin lights went out and people were sleeping. The giant next to him was snoring loudly, but the real difficulty was his enormous bulk crushing Adam against the sidewall of the plane. Adam pushed against him with all his strength. He finally toppled in the other direction and was hanging over into the aisle. Passengers coming up the aisle had to pass the man sideways. Some bumped against him flopping him back onto Adam.

This back and forth went on for an hour. The next time Adam pushed the man he said in his sleep, "Gott im Himmel," which Adam knew meant "God in Heaven" or, as Americans might say, "Oh, my God!" Adam thought it was he who deserved God's intervention, not his enormous seatmate. He would have liked to utter in return another German word he knew: *lebensraum,* more room. Lebensraum had been the word that "justified" the Nazi invasion of every country within reach. But it was Adam who needed some lebensraum just then.

With that "Gott im Himmel," this man was almost certainly German, and Adam couldn't help thinking that, with his crushing size, the Germans were still abusing Jews every chance they got. The man looked to be fifty or sixty—though it was difficult to judge his age because of his bulk. He would probably have been between twenty and thirty during the war. Adam wondered whether he had been a soldier, S.S., Gestapo, or a concentration camp guard. Given his looks he must have done something evil during the war.

But Adam knew looks could be deceiving. What if the fat giant, unattractive though he might be, had actually been one of the rare good Germans? Or just because he said "Gott im Himmel," did that mean he was definitely German? Didn't Austrians speak German?

I've got to stop this, Adam thought. I'm going to be in the Berlin airport soon. Will I be unable to relate to any German besides Zoe without knowing the full specifics of their past?

Even if his enormous seatmate had not been a Nazi, he now committed a sin beyond anyone's powers of forgiveness. He let out a trumpet blast of a fart. It would likely have blown up a person of lesser size and scattered them about the airplane, if it didn't bring the plane down first. Some of the people across the aisle who were awake snickered and looked in their direction. Hopefully, none suspected Adam of the crime. He thought of standing and pointing to the perpetrator.

The Germans onboard could not wait till he got to Berlin; they wanted to gas him en route. Whether this guy had been a Nazi or not, he was living proof that all Germans had obnoxious qualities that sooner or later would reveal themselves. But, then again, there was Zoe. Yes, there certainly was Zoe.

Requiring some relief from his seatmate, Adam tried to get up from his seat, but it was hopeless. There wasn't an inch between the enormous German and the seat in front of him. Also, given his great girth, it was impossible for Adam to step over him into the aisle without pulling a muscle or giving himself a hernia. If the man hadn't fully occupied both arm rests, it might have been possible to step from one to the other and then drop down into the aisle, but that too was impossible. He finally stepped from one of the man's knees to the other. Perhaps those knees were so padded with fat he would not feel it, but he did emit another "Gott im Himmel."

Being out in the aisle was delightful after being trapped in his seat by that tub of lard. Each step was liberating. Walking back towards the rest room, he looked for an empty seat into which he might sink. Nothing. Every seat was filled.

In the rest room, he used a damp paper towel to remove, as best he could, the mashed potatoes and gravy stain from his crotch. Concerned his fellow passengers might think he had peed his pants, he decided to hang out with the stewardesses in the back of the plane while his pants dried. Anything to delay returning to his seat.

The stewardess who had brought the giant to his seat asked if he was having a pleasant flight.

"Yes," he said, "except for my seatmate."

"Ah," she said, "are you the man who kindly let us unite the older couple?"

"Yes," Adam said, "but I hadn't counted on the man who replaced the woman."

"He is rather large," she admitted.

"Rather," Adam replied.

"But he was very nice giving up his seat for the woman."

Adam didn't reply. He waited in vain for the stewardess to recognize his own considerably greater sacrifice, but it wasn't forthcoming.

He soon began to feel he was intruding on the stewardesses' space. Though he would have preferred to go anywhere else, it was time to return to his seat. But before doing so, he walked up and down the aisle several times. It felt good moving his body. Then, instead of walking from knee to knee, he crawled over the gigantic, poisonous German who, still fast asleep, emitted yet another "Gott im Himmel."

"Yeah, well fuck you," Adam whispered directly into the man's face before falling into his own seat. He hoped the man heard him and understood at least that much English.

Adam may have briefly slept at some point—he wasn't sure. Light was now coming through the plastic window cover next to his seat. He pushed it up and saw that it was daylight; perhaps it had been daylight for some time. Also, they were no longer over the ocean; there was land below. The Captain announced that they were beginning their initial descent into the airport.

The flight approached Berlin above a couple of lakes. Were these the Wannsee lakes? They looked like them from the maps he had studied of Greater Berlin. Wannsee was where the "final solution" had been planned in a villa. Final solution to what? What was the problem, exactly? Adam smiled to himself thinking that his death and that of all Jews everywhere would have been someone's final solution. Perhaps those Jews who had not been swept up in the Nazis' killing machine should have committed suicide to help with the "solution." The least we could do, he chuckled sardonically to himself.

Landing smoothly, the plane taxied towards the terminal. On the building was written in large letters ARBEIT MACHT FREI. "No," Adam told himself, "get a grip." It said, WILLKOMMEN IM BERLIN.

CHAPTER 13

Adam followed the huge German as he slowly lumbered down the aisle. It was impossible to get around him in the narrow passageway. The tiny, white plastic carry-on in his meaty hand made him look even larger. It occurred to Adam that he and the German had not exchanged a single word during the entire flight. They had never even said hello, so there was no point in saying goodbye. In any case, Adam's sentiments were more along the lines of good riddance.

In the terminal, the Danish couple caught up with them and thanked Adam in English for helping unite them on the plane and thanked his enormous seatmate in what he took to be German. Adam was a trifle disappointed that the Danes, the good Danes, could speak German—if that's what it was—not to mention that they had inflicted the giant German on him. Was it possible the husband had been even more interested in getting rid of him than in having his wife join him? Nevertheless, Adam lied and repeated what he had said earlier, "My pleasure." The German merely grunted.

It occurred to Adam that the enormous German had served a certain purpose. His fear of Germany and everything German had been mitigated by the utter disgust engendered by this man. No one could better illustrate that the Germans weren't, and never could have been, the master race. Why hadn't the Germans themselves seen that? Hitler was a little punk—not German but Austrian, Himmler was butt ugly, Goebbels had a club foot and looked like a cadaver, and Goering was almost as fat as Adam's seatmate. Next time, he said to himself, you master race Germans will be lucky if we let you eat our shit.

Nevertheless, he was nervous in the terminal. Paranoia slowly crept over him, enveloping him like low lying fog. He seemed to be hyperventilating and could feel his heart racing. It would be just his luck to have a heart attack in the Berlin airport. The Nazis would get him after all.

He felt faint as he went through Passport Control. It didn't help that the officer was checking his face to compare it with the passport picture—or did he have something else in mind? The loud *cachung* noise as he stamped the passport made Adam jump. And what was the meaning of the man's smile? Was it a friendly smile? Or was it, "Gotcha!"

Downstairs, Adam waited for his suitcase at a carousel. A burly man was helping with luggage. He looked at Adam. Gestapo? Would he want to see Adam's papers?

Cut it out, Adam told himself. It's just an airport. His paranoia kept returning and receding, like waves on a beach. Who were those guys in uniform over there? Were they pretending to be airport employees? What were they talking about? Why were all the security cameras in the terminal pointed in his direction? Even now he was being monitored in a dark room by the S.S. They were recording his every breath.

Stop it! he said to himself. The S.S. doesn't exist anymore. The only S.S. is Social Security in the U.S. Couldn't America have come up with a better name for that program than Social Security, so it wouldn't have those terrible initials, S.S.? Whenever Adam was asked to supply his S.S. number, he cringed. He fantasized saying, "Fuck you and your S.S." He never did but always wished he had. After all, why did he and others have to be constantly reminded of Nazi Germany by a United States government agency?

Still, Zoe lived here. He had to remember that he came here to see Zoe. Without looking further at the baggage handler, he collected his suitcase and, dreamlike, moved across the terminal. It felt like he was watching a silent movie of himself. Was this terminal weird or was it just him? He felt disassociated, as if he was back in his dream at the Imperial Hotel in Indiana.

The Muzak whined like an exhausted insect late in season. Adam endeavored to pick out the tune. My God, he realized, it's "My Funny Valentine." The Germans had taken over "My Funny Valentine." Or was it the other way around. He preferred not to attribute romantic sentiments to Germans. But then there was Zoe…

He passed a long line of stores; some of the same stores one found in American airports. There was also a newsstand with books, newspapers, and magazines mostly in German. Lots of skin magazines were freely displayed. They also had the *International Herald Tribune*, so Adam bought one, paying in dollars. Nothing remarkable on the front page. What did he expect, a headline saying, "JEW SPOTTED IN BERLIN AIRPORT?" He realized that he had just spent some money in Germany—something he had told Zoe at the Grand Canyon he would never do. But wasn't he staying in a hotel? That was real money, so to hell with concerning himself about the purchase of a newspaper.

Next to the newsstand was what appeared to be a German fast food restaurant where he thought he would have a hamburger. But then he thought, hamburgers must be called that because they're named for Hamburg, Germany's second largest city. He had eaten hamburgers all his life, but he was damned if he would eat one in Germany. A frankfurter would also be suspect here. It was probably named for Frankfurt—though he reluctantly admitted to himself that so was the Jewish justice of the United States Supreme Court, Felix Frankfurter. There were other things on the menu such as Currywurst and Bouletten, but he didn't know what they were.

He went back to the newsstand and bought some American candy. He loved having a justification for eating nothing but candy for lunch—Peanut M&M's and a Hershey chocolate bar with almonds. They were mixed in with what must have been German candy near the cash register.

Underway again, he came to a strange looking store with its window lit with pink and purple fluorescent lights that spelled out in English, "PLAYLAND." In the window were two plastic blown up naked women, their mouths and vaginas perpetually open and available. Was this some kind of avant-garde conceptual art? Adam peered in the front door of the store. No art in there; it was exactly what it appeared to be: a porno store, right here in the airport. Sex toys of all kinds were for sale, including shelves of plastic, vibrating penises. Two women seemed to be shopping among the penises. In the back, a thin, dark curtain, behind which there appeared to be peepshow booths and the shadows of men making their way from one to the other.

Is this what Germans did between planes, hang out in adult shops? Was a porno store in an airport a sign of extreme liberalism or of rank perversion? Later, Adam would learn that prostitution was, while not technically legal, freely available in West Berlin. Maybe when the Germans weren't killing people, they obsessively turned to sex. Maybe they had actually been followers of Freud—Jewish or not—in his notion that the two great forces in human thinking are *thanatos* and *eros,* death and sex. The Nazi era was all thanatos. Could it be that Germany had flipped and was now all eros? It seemed the Germans did not do things by halves. Adam recalled the slogan opposing the Vietnam War: Make love, not war. Maybe all of Germany had now turned into a Teutonic Woodstock.

Still, a porno store in an airport? Weren't airports family oriented? What did parents tell their children when they passed by that window with the two life-size plastic women—and what kind of desperate soul might want a plastic woman? The guy over on the right, probably. He was perusing the packages of plastic women, perhaps deciding on the one he found most attractive. Blond or brunette? The guy kept looking behind him, perhaps making sure nobody he knew was observing him as he examined the plastic women. He glanced at Adam where he was standing in the doorway. Adam looked away.

Would the man board his plane with a plastic woman in his carry-on? Then, when the plane reached cruising altitude and the captain turned off the seat belt signs, would he casually stroll to the back of the plane with the innocuous plastic bag under his arm, go into one of the rest rooms, inflate the plastic woman, and fuck her standing up? No worries about turbulence. In fact, turbulence might even add to the occasion.

Then after letting out all of the air and returning her to the plastic bag, he would stroll back to his seat looking perfectly proper though imagining, with some satisfaction, this might qualify him for membership in the mile high club—though slightly troubled that maybe it had to be a real woman with whom you had sex in an airplane rest room for admission to the club. Adam found the man considering the purchase of a blow-up woman in an airport hilarious.

His paranoia briefly lifted but returned as he realized that Germany was quite capable of flipping back from eros to thanatos at any time. The porno store, like everything in the airport, had an air of unreality to it. The terminal was also too brightly lit and antiseptic, as if they did surgery and medical experiments in the rooms off the main hall. No doubt that was where they strapped Jews down, put duct tape over their mouths, and removed their organs one by one without anesthesia.

What about the man behind the newspaper on the plastic bench? Why was his face hidden except for one eye? Was that his eye boring into Adam's back as he moved further down the concourse?

And why was there an immense Hasid standing in his path, so black in all this whiteness? To Adam, the Hasidim were evidence that Jews, like all religious groups, produce their share of weirdos. Except for the fact the Nazis would have killed him five minutes after they killed a Hasid because they so obviously stood out, Adam felt little, if any, affinity with the Hasidim.

Was this guy a real Hasid or had he been posted there to monitor Adam? What better disguise for a Nazi than to dress as a Hasid? Was this man's earlocks real or part of a wig, and was he actually swaying in prayer or speaking into a tiny microphone in his lapel? "American Jew at four o'clock." Any moment now a troop of S.S. were going to march across the tile floor and arrest Adam. They had a gas chamber attached to the airport. "Und you don't even haf to go outside." No more messy cattle cars. Fly the Jews in. Gas chambers for the jet set.

Knowing he was coming, the Nazis probably cleaned up the terminal, replaced all the swastika banners with those rather pretty, unthreatening tri-color flags of black, red, and gold, and swept up every trace of bones and hair and teeth, and all those tattered yellow Stars of David. These remains were probably now interred beneath the very floor on which Adam was walking.

Indeed, there was fresh tile work fifty feet to his left. The corral of plastic cones surrounding it suggested a recent "repair," but the black sign on the barriers, *VERBOTEN*, revealed its true nature.

This was another word Adam knew—like *actung*—from movies about Nazis. Of course, any German word agitated Adam, even Oktoberfest. Wasn't Oktoberfest when Nazis drank beer and sang the "Horst Wessel Song"? But verboten was right up there with actung in its murderous possibilities. Slowly but surely everything German Jews needed to live decently had been verboten—jobs, education, recreation, telephones, radios, their businesses, and their professions. They could only shop for food during limited hours. They even weren't allowed to have pets. And then being alive itself became verboten. Zoe said German was a language like any other, but the verboten sign made Adam think he was definitely behind enemy lines.

He passed endless Lufthansa counters, each with lines of passengers. He imagined these people as standing on the platform at Auschwitz, grimly awaiting Mengele's decision on their fate: passengers for planes that will only experience continuous, violent turbulence to the right; passengers for planes that will crash and kill you to the left.

Up ahead was a sky bridge to the hotel. Adam turned to see if anyone was following him. Nobody. But they were surely too clever to let themselves be seen. They had probably planted a bug in his suitcase and knew exactly where he was at all times.

I've got to stop this, he said to himself for the tenth time. This is just an airport terminal. It could be anywhere in the world. It just happens to be in Germany.

Now he was on the motorized walkway of the sky bridge, sailing along on the River Styx with Hades just ahead. The music? Was it being played by a few Jewish musicians—Strauss waltzes—forced by the Nazis to trick observers like the International Red Cross into believing all was well at the concentration camp, everyone happy and well cared for—it was practically a resort.

Stop it, he again said to himself. It's the same Muzak as before, this time "Days of Wine and Roses."

He was swept into the lobby of the hotel where the desk clerk was full of smiles. Were they genuine smiles or did all those bright teeth suggest something sinister?

"Herr Levin," he said, "welcome to our hotel."

"If you don't mind," Adam said, "don't call me Herr. Mister, please."

"Of course, Mister Levin. No Herrs." He laughed uproariously. What was so funny? Adam wondered. Okay, so Herr meant Mister. But Adam was damned if he'd let people address him as Herr, as in Herr Hitler and Herr Goebbels. If you let them say "Herr," the next minute they'd be saying "Heil." Fuck that. He managed a wan smile. Better not to stir up the natives.

"And will you be paying in dollars or Deutsche Marks?"

"Dollars, credit card" Adam said emphatically. He preferred not to possess any German money, as if it might give him a disease or rot his wallet.

Having signed the register and with plastic key now in hand, Adam moved to the elevator. The song was now "Moon River," his absolute favorite. Was that Frank Sinatra or Andy Williams? Probably Sinatra. The Jersey accent came through when he sang "riveeeer." But what was it with these Germans and American pop music? Why didn't they get their own pop music?

Although he felt ridiculous doing it, once in his room he searched his suitcase to see whether, indeed, a bug had been planted there. What about the lining? Could a listening device have been sewn in? He felt around for a lump. "Stop it," he said out loud. "Stop it or you're going to go crazy."

But what about the mirror? Could they be observing him through the mirror the way he and his wife had been observed through a two-way mirror during their unhelpful sex therapy? Wasn't it the mirror that was used by Big Brother's minions in Orwell's *1984* to observe Winston Smith or was it a television set? Adam turned on the television just to insure it was indeed a television set. A brace of German transvestites were being interviewed on a talk show. There it was again, thanatos or eros: Germans were either more tyrannical or more open minded than other people. Never in-between.

Adam decided to check the drawers in the dresser as well. They were empty except for two Gideon Bibles, one in English, the other in German. With its Gothic script, the German version looked like a bunch of death certificates. Throughout the Jewish part of the German Bible the word *Juden* appeared over and over. Adam knew that

Juden meant Jews in German, but he could only think of it in terms of smashed shop windows, torture, and death camps. It made him also think of *Judenrein*, being rid of the Jews, to which the Nazis had been so dedicated.

Enough! Adam said to himself. With the seven hours difference, he had arrived at eleven in the morning in Germany, which meant for him it was four. Up all night, he was exhausted and wanted to feel fresh when he saw Zoe, who was scheduled to arrive after work at five-thirty. Nevertheless, from his bedroom window, he briefly watched planes taking off and landing, mostly Lufthansas with dark blue tails and yellow circles in the middle of them with dark blue flying cranes. Seeing so many sparkling Lufthansas, a tribute to Germany's affluence, offended him.

Now to bed, he told himself. He called the hotel reception desk, left a wake-up call for four forty-five with the "Herr" guy and went to sleep.

CHAPTER 14

Adam dreamed as he slept in his hotel room, yet all he remembered was something about the Nazis and the patients of the Beth Jacob Home for the Incurables. They were dancing with one another. He remembered feeling nauseous. He remembered screaming. Or thought he was screaming, but it was actually the phone ringing. The front desk was calling as he had requested. Caught up on his rest, Adam's mind was still foggy. Zoe had been right: he was stuck on the Nazis; he had to get them out of his mind. The incurables too.

He began to feel better in the shower, especially when he began to sing. Though he was unhappy with what he considered German expropriation of American songs he heard moving through the airport and in the elevator, he was singing those very songs now.

At five-fifteen, dressed in carefully selected clothes—informal but not too informal—he was again looking out the window at the planes. The Lufthansas were a lot better to look at than before. Perhaps he had gotten used to them.

It had been understood that Zoe would call him from the lobby when she arrived at five-thirty, but there was a knock on his door. Who could it be? Not Zoe yet. Though if it was, it meant she was so eager to see him and arrived early, a good sign. Not to mention that she had come to his room—which offered all sorts of possibilities. Adam went to the door and peered through the peep hole.

Zoe was standing there, beautiful as ever—maybe more so. Adam opened the door to a whole new Zoe. She was wearing a floral dress with lace around the collar and cuffs, and she had on high heels. His hiking companion at the Grand Canyon now looked like a lady. No shorts, no hiking boots, no braid—even though part of him missed all that. Her blond hair was down, framing her face and making her eyes even more spectacular. She also appeared more sophisticated and, if this was possible, sexier. Did she have makeup on? If so, did lesbians put on makeup for each other or was this for him?

Adam didn't know what to do. Here was Zoe at his hotel room door. He wanted to kiss her—at least that. Lips? Cheek? Put his arms around her? What?

Zoe decided for them both. "Adam," she said with her lovely smile, advancing into his room and putting her arms around him. She momentarily rested her head on his shoulder and then lightly kissed him on the lips. Adam wondered what it meant. Lightly, yes, but on the lips?

Where was this going? Adam wondered. Was this a repeat of the Grand Canyon with Zoe claiming she was a lesbian but sitting on his bed with only a towel on? He knew what he wanted to do, wanted it so badly he ached, but what was he supposed to do?

She said, "It's nice to see you alone for a moment, which is why I came up. A quiet moment to tell you that I love you. But I think we'd better go downstairs to the restaurant now. If I stay here another minute, I'll violate my promise to Annika. I mustn't, especially if I want her to love you too."

"Annika love me too?"

"Yes."

"And do I have to love her as well?"

"You will."

In the restaurant they managed to secure a quiet corner table. Adam pulled out a chair for Zoe, something that didn't seem appropriate when she was in her hiking gear at the Grand Canyon. She sat and straightened her skirt. It was now dark outside, though they could still make out planes taking off and hear the roar of their engines.

"So, you've come to Germany at last," Zoe said.

"Well, to the airport."

"And I can't talk you into coming into town?"

"No, Zoe, I can't. Almost like you couldn't stay in my room another minute."

"You know what might have happened if we had done that," she said with a little laugh.

"Yes, but one can always hope," he said, smiling. "Things change. I said I would never come to Germany, not even to change planes, but here I am. And look: there we are reflected in the window, just like at the canyon. Old times."

"Old times," she said with that inimitable smile. "And you fly to India tomorrow?

"Yes, and I'm itching and aching from the eight different shots they gave me and the malaria pills I'm taking."

Zoe picked up a menu and joked, "I'll have what you're having"

"First some wine," Adam said. He didn't know German wines, so he ordered a Spanish Rioja.

"I'm going to need wine," Zoe said. "Maybe a lot of wine. There's something I need to talk with you about, and I'm nervous."

"You're not going to ask me to marry you?" he said lightly, though with a touch of hope. "Don't be nervous. The answer is yes!"

"If I were to marry a man, you would be the only candidate," Zoe said. "No, I will not be discussing marriage but something equally intimate."

"Equally intimate? That sounds promising. I'm dying to know what it is."

Zoe laughed. "Let's have some wine first. And eat. Then we'll talk."

They split a salad and then both had coq au vin over rice. French food in a German airport hotel accompanied by a second bottle of the Spanish wine. The world was indeed becoming smaller, and like it or not, Germany was in it.

The waitress cleared their table. They ordered dessert, and while waiting, Zoe said, "Do you remember at the Grand Canyon saying you wanted to marry me, wanted to have children with me?"

"I feel the same way now."

"And do you remember when I told you on the phone that Annika and I had decided to have children?"

"Sure, I remember."

"And that we were converting to Judaism and would raise our children Jewish?"

"Yes," he said. "Welcome to the tribe."

"Well, we want you to be the father of our children."

Adam sat there stunned. Unconsciously he was shredding the paper napkin in his lap with his fingers.

Zoe waited for him to say something but hurried on when he didn't. "There is no man that I would prefer. Nor Annika. In fact, she's the one who suggested it. She knew the best way for her to fully recover from my love affair with you was to, in a sense, *join it*. I've told her everything I know about you. She's read some of your books. She admires you."

"Have you considered adoption?"

"Yes, but we want to know pregnancy, want to give birth, want the children to be biologically ours, and want to experience what women have always experienced."

"How exactly would you and I do this?"

"Not just you and I. You and I and Annika."

"Woah, this is kinky. You're proposing a threesome? But I don't even know Annika. I'm not a prude, but with all due respect…"

"I'm not talking about having sex."

"Then what are you talking about?

"Your seed. I care so deeply about you, and Annika, without even having met you, has begun to feel the same. We want the father of our children to be the same man, and there isn't anyone on the planet we would prefer to you."

"Same man? Sounds like a kind of adultery. What about a sperm bank?"

"We don't want a stranger's sperm. That would almost repeat how I came into the world when my mother was gang raped by the Russians. We want to know the father of our children. Perhaps he would care about them too. If not, we would always know who he was and care about him. It would be his seed that created them, not the seed of an unknown man."

"Don't you have any gay male friends? I hear some gays are very keen on being fathers. If a gay friend was the father, you would know who he was."

"We do have some gay male friends, but they're not you. When I told Annika that you're the only man I've ever loved, she was generous. She said, 'Then he should be the father of our children.' *Our* children she said."

"But how would this be done exactly?" Adam asked.

"Your sperm in a teacup"

"A teacup? Not a mustache cup?"

"What?"

"Too complicated to explain," Adam continued. "And?"

"We insert it with a turkey baster. We read about this in a magazine article on lesbians having children. We lubricate the baster. With a turkey baster the sperm can be put right up against the cervix—and a woman would be actually sure of conception. Better than a penis—present company excepted, of course. I suspect you and a turkey baster would be neck and neck as to who was the better impregnator."

"Well," Adam said, "it's comforting that I'd be competitive with a turkey baster."

"And you Americans being so devoted to Thanksgiving, a turkey baster might almost have patriotic connotations."

"Yes," Adam replied. "I sometimes wish the turkey was our national bird instead of the bald eagle. Less bellicose."

"Remember, the babies would technically be half-American. And Jewish, like their mothers, and with a Jewish father, too—a Jewish father we love."

"But what about menstrual cycles? Ovulation? I don't mean to pry, but…"

"Annika and I are on the same cycle. This often happens when women live together: they get on the same cycle and ovulate at the same time."

"So?"

"So, we would want you to come to Berlin for a week during the time we would be ovulating."

"And?"

"And every day for about five days you would—how do you Americans say it?"

"Jerk off."

"Is that the same as masturbate?"

Adam assured her that it was. "Sometimes they call it autoeroticism. I used to think it had something to do with having sexual feelings for automobiles. But no automobile can compare in its erotic appeal to a teacup." He laughed and stopped shredding his napkin. Not wishing to reveal how anxious he had been, he let its remnants drop to the floor and brushed off his pants. "But are you sure this would be an adult, consenting teacup, that no charges would be brought against me by the International Society for Teacup Rights?"

Zoe laughed too. "You would be willing to do it?"

"I'll think hard about it. You've got to admit it's pretty weird. Besides, what about the legalities?"

"Taken care of. As you know, I'm a lawyer. Annika too. Also, we consulted a specialist in the field. German law allows drawing up papers that would relieve you of all responsibility, financially or otherwise. And the children would be German—unless you wanted them to have dual citizenship; that too could be arranged. Either way you could see these children whenever you liked and could be listed as their father—also if you'd like. I want my child to know he or she had a father and know his name and that he lives in America. And even if you never came to Germany again, the children would grow up with pictures of their father on the walls of our home. Unlike me, they would not have to say they had no father."

"Well," said Adam, "I did dream of having children with you, so I guess this is something. But I've never laid eyes on Annika, and I'm still in love with you. I'd enjoy you carrying our baby and watching you nurse that baby with those beautiful breasts of yours. I can hardly think of anything more sensual." Zoe was blushing. "But why would I want to father a child with Annika?"

"I can't swear you'll love Annika when you meet her. But she already loves you and wants to have your baby. Doesn't that count for something?"

"Well, I guess I should be flattered but, frankly, including Annika in this feels weird, almost perverted."

"You won't feel that way when you meet Annika. She's a wonderful person. If you love me, you'll love Annika too."

"Well, anything's possible. But how about a compromise? You and I make love every night I'm in Berlin, and I jerk off into the teacup for Annika? We must have been making love three times a day at the Grand Canyon. There's millions of sperm every time, and it just takes one good one."

"I can't, Adam. As attractive as that still sounds to the part of me you know, Annika is my partner for life. If the law ever allows it, I will marry Annika. You would be our first choice to sign the papers as witness. Better than that: to walk us down the aisle, one on each arm. Annika already loves you as the possible father of her child, and she hasn't even met you. Doesn't that mean something to you?"

"I suppose. But why can't she get sperm from another man?"

"As I said, Annika and I want the same man as the father of our children. She and I will share that forever—as will the children. Something, also, we would share with you. In fact, we would want the children to have the same last name, not Annika's or mine but yours. With your permission, of course."

"You mean they would have the last name, Levin?"

"If you didn't mind."

"It's flattering." Adam exclaimed. "But even if I did all this, I couldn't promise to come back to Germany."

"That would be up to you. But these would be your children. You might like to see them once in a while, take pride in them. And whatever else you do, if you marry, even have children with another woman, Annika and I and our children would be family too, as much or as little as you desired."

Cappuccinos and a thick slice of seven-layer cake to share arrived, and they held off on continuing the conversation until the waitress left and they were alone again.

Zoe went on. "Adam, you said on the phone that you would do anything for me. Now I'm asking. I'm asking this out of love—both for you and for Annika. Think of it in humanitarian terms: you would be doing something wonderful for two women. Also, at the Grand Canyon you admitted your frustration at having been on the sidelines during the Holocaust—even though you were just a child. Here is your chance to personally bring new German Jews to life."

"And if I agreed, when would this happen?

"I would give you our fertile dates for the next few months. You would come to Germany for one of those dates, whichever was convenient for you."

"You've really figured this out."

"Annika and I have talked about this for weeks. That's why I couldn't speak with you when you first phoned: I wanted to check with Annika one more time. I had to make sure she was—how do you say it?—on board."

"Phew," Adam said. "This is something I really have to think about. And, obviously, if I agreed, I would be coming into the city, coming into Germany. Not just the airport—Germany."

"Yes, but Annika and I are Germany too. You would stay with us. We have a guest room. Someday it will be the nursery.

"It is time to give up this unhealthy obsession, Adam. The Nazis are long gone. There are many good Germans, good people, kind people. And the very best, kindest, and sweetest would be the children we produced together, you and two women who would always love you."

Adam didn't know what to say. He looked about the room and at the planes outside roaring by. He looked at Zoe who was waiting expectantly. Finally, he said, "This is the strangest offer I've ever had in my life. It's like a fairy tale."

"Sometimes strangest is best."

"If I ever marry again, I would have to tell the woman that I already have children."

"Yes," Zoe said. "And she would understand if you told her the whole story, from the Grand Canyon to the birth of our children. Otherwise, she would not be the right woman to marry."

They sat in silence for a while. It was late. The waitress had cleared the dessert and coffee cups off the table.

Adam called for the bill. "Not this time," Zoe said. "In Germany, you are my guest."

She paid the bill, and Adam said, "Come on. I'll walk you to your car."

"My car is in the parking lot. You'll have to come outside. You will have to actually set foot in Germany, not just the airport terminal," she said, teasing him.

"Well," Adam said, "maybe it's time I did exactly that."

Later, in his room, Adam thought of a conversation he had with his wife late in their marriage. "You should get a vasectomy," she said.

"Why?"

"Because we're obviously not going to have children. And I can't go through another misery like the two times I got pregnant and lost the babies. Never."

"Then get your tubes tied."

"Always it's the woman," she said. "Everyone in my group thinks you should get a vasectomy."

Adam didn't answer. First, he didn't like that his wife discussed the most intimate details of his anatomy with her women friends, but he was also damned if he would mutilate his body on a whim of hers. When it came to abortion, he believed one hundred percent in a woman's right to choose. He believed the same about a man getting a vasectomy; nobody owed anyone else a vasectomy.

And now there was this peculiar but magical proposal of Zoe's and Annika's. He was far from sure he would do it, but, as he fell asleep, he smiled knowing he could.

CHAPTER 15

In India, all Adam could think of was Germany—Germany, Zoe, and Annika. Did he wish to father children with them? And in such a…well, he could hardly put a name to it…*clinical* way. Perhaps, but that hardly included the strong emotions he was feeling. Besides, he would be going into a country he hated (or perhaps he was ready to say had hated?) to spend five days to a week in Berlin jerking off into a teacup while the women ovulated.

India was the strangest country he had ever visited—dead people on the sidewalk, traffic bumper to bumper at all times with horns honking nonstop, peddlers trying to sell him cobras in woven straw baskets, beggars harassing him wherever he went, audiences at his talks wagging their heads side to side in approval instead of up and down, lizards and giant bugs on his hotel room ceiling, everything brightly colored—food, clothing, temples—and cows wandering the streets as dogs and cats do in other countries. The safest, sometimes the only, way to cross the street (the box at every intersection being blocked) was to walk between a pair of strolling cows. Traffic miraculously got out of the way then. If an Indian driver hit a pedestrian it was no big deal. But if he hit a cow, he might be beaten to death by a Hindu mob.

Yes, a strange country, but what he was considering doing in Germany was stranger still. He wanted Zoe but couldn't have her. The thought of her carrying his child did have its appeal, as did the fact that, of all the men on the planet, only his sperm was desired. Thinking of her beautiful body with his baby inside it, he found himself with an erection. At first he thought, that's perverted. But then he thought, why not?

Returning from India he found a letter from Germany awaiting him. There was a brief note signed by both Zoe and Annika saying, "We love you, Adam." Enclosed were pictures of both of them alone and together. Annika was leaner, rangier, more angular and a bit taller than Zoe. She had on jogging clothes and bright yellow sneakers. She looked like a runner, but a beautiful runner. Soft brown eyes, a bright smile, long black hair. They both looked feminine and sweet. In any case, after his Grand Canyon experience, he resisted all such categorizations of people. Zoe was a lesbian, but she was *his* lesbian, and no label could do her loveliness justice. Also, Adam had to admit if he met Annika instead of Zoe at the Grand Canyon, based on looks alone, he would have followed her into the gift shop too.

There was also a picture of the two of them sitting at a table studying with their rabbi, who had written on the back of it, "I look forward to meeting you, Adam. I suspect you are a good man and a good Jew." The rabbi, no doubt Reform, was young and quite handsome—nothing like the Orthodox rabbi with his long, moldy beard who had given Adam his bar mitzvah training at the Beth Abraham Home for the Incurables. He was wearing jeans and a denim jacket in the picture and looked like a cool guy. You would never imagine he was a rabbi.

And it sounded like the project had the rabbi's blessing, not just the converting but the baby making too. "Jewish credit," in addition to everything else, awaited Adam in Berlin. He rarely attended synagogue, but now he could tell himself he was doing something for his people.

Still, the main appeal was intimate contact with Zoe even of a distant kind. And, as for Annika, he had read somewhere that men sleep around more than women because of an innate desire to spread their seed and maybe because they don't get pregnant. Annika would certainly be a means of spreading his seed. He felt a certain macho pride in impregnating two beautiful women. He would be the Johnny Appleseed of…well, whatever it was.

And he could do it without being unfaithful to anyone—get two women pregnant while doing them a favor. Further, as Zoe had assured him, he would have no responsibility whatsoever for the children other than what he might, in time, desire.

Was there a defect in his thinking? Was there a hitch? He had just turned forty; it was time he had children. And the children these two women would produce would likely be children to be proud of…and Jews, members of his tribe. He would be helping to replenish the race, and in the precise place where every effort had been made to annihilate it. What better way to play his part in overcoming what the Nazis had done?

Would he prefer girls or boys? One of each would be perfect. But he wanted Zoe's child to be a girl—a new human being who reminded him of her and literally emerged from her body. If he couldn't have Zoe, he could have a little Zoe.

He phoned Zoe. "I'll do it," he said. "Give me the ovulation calendar for you and Annika over the next few months."

Zoe was overjoyed. She promised to call back with the dates within a few hours. "And Adam," she added, "I love you now more than ever."

When Zoe called back with the dates, Adam saw one set conformed perfectly with his university's mid-March spring break: two free weekends and the week between them, nine days in all. He could arrive the day before the women's fertile periods and rest up before "going to work." He laughed to himself; he might just need some rest.

Zoe said she would meet his flight and take him into the city. "First order of business: you and Annika must get to know each other."

"I'm a little anxious about that," he admitted.

"She's anxious too," she replied. "Imagine meeting a man for the first time, and he's going to father your child."

"Not the way things usually go," Adam said.

"Nothing about this is the way things usually go," Zoe said. "Maybe that's why it's so wonderful."

Adam could hardly concentrate on his work at the university during the weeks preceding his trip to Germany—a trip whose only purpose was to impregnate two women. He found himself rather enthralled with the project. Pursuing other women, for the present, seemed gratuitous. Besides, he thought, maybe he should save up his sperm and arrive fully loaded.

He had read somewhere that men who wore boxer shorts were more fertile than those who wore briefs. Briefs kept one's equipment fully encircled and too close to the body, too warm. With boxers your balls were ideally kept one degree cooler than the rest of your body for maximum sperm production. Boxers kept things cool, let it all hang out. There was talk that the sperm count of younger men was now lower than when Adam was their age because, some medical people believed, most wore briefs or, as one of Adam's students referred to them, "tidy whities." Adam couldn't help but feel superior to younger men and their lower sperm counts.

He bought a half dozen pairs of white boxer shorts. White seemed the right color—clean, bright. If he was going to do this thing, he wanted to do it right.

He also read that exercise raised one's testosterone level, so he went to the university gym every day. He was in training for the sexual olympics, the reproductive sweepstakes.

He imagined conversations with male university colleagues. So, what are you doing spring break? I'm going to Germany to get two women pregnant. Sure you don't need some help?

Sometimes he found himself looking forward to the trip with great enthusiasm. Other times he wondered if he was making a mistake that would haunt him forever. Not only would he be going into Berlin for a week, he would be entangling his life with Germany and Germans forever and producing children for whom he would feel at least some responsibility—even though that wasn't a required part of the deal.

Once he picked up the phone in his shabby apartment to call Zoe and cancel the trip but then gently set it down again. He would go if only for the sheer adventure of it. You only live once, he told himself, so what the hell? He knew that if he didn't do it he was certain to be sorry. He might be equally sorry or more so if he did do it, but he might feel quite the reverse: enthralled, joyful. He wasn't a betting man, but he figured the percentages were on the side of doing it. Go for it he told himself. He had never considered himself a cautious man. Why start now?

He booked a round-trip flight. This time he chose Lufthansa. What the hell, he thought. If I'm doing this, I might as well go all the way.

He had to admit: the Lufthansa flight was very pleasant. The stewardesses were friendly and easy to look at. And the German they spoke was soft and unlike what he'd always imagined the language to sound like—*achtung, verboten* and all that. The food was certainly better than what he had experienced on Pan American during the previous trip. Everything on the plane seemed civilized. And there was no giant in the seat next to him, crushing him all the way to Berlin. In fact, a very pretty young woman was sitting there. He thought of initiating conversation with her during dinner but didn't quite have the nerve. Now she was sleeping. Soon he was too.

He began to pay more attention to his seatmate when the lights came on in the morning and breakfast was being served. Her name was Clare. She had light brown hair in a pageboy haircut with one ear exposed. He had always been attracted to the one ear exposed look. It was a kind of ear striptease, which left just enough mystery about the covered one while the exposed one was inviting and vulnerable.

He was also attracted by the way Clare's hair flicked side to side when she spoke in her animated fashion and the way she delicately threaded her hair back behind the exposed ear with two fingers. She had deep brown eyes with long lashes. When she got up to go to the rest room, Adam turned in his seat and followed her with his eyes. She had on a form fitting, charcoal colored dress. He liked the back of her as much as the front and enjoyed watching her walk. She was petite but exuded strength and determination. You could tell a lot about a woman by the way she walked. Lord, she was really pretty!

He particularly noticed her slim waist and thought of what it would be like to put his arm around it. If he had to decide, that's what he liked best about a woman—a slim waist and then that graceful flaring out at the hips. Men just came straight down. He was still thinking about her waist and hips when she returned and seated herself next to him in a graceful manner. Even the way she sat down—feminine, sweet—enticed him.

He learned that Clare was actually a graduate student in Sociology at Adam's own university. She had a grant and was going to Berlin for research on her Ph.D. dissertation.

"What on?" Adam asked.

"Tentative title: 'The Resurgence of Judaism in Contemporary Germany.'"

"You're Jewish?"

"No, I'm an atheist, but all my friends are Jewish. I guess you could call me a *Judeophile*."

"Well, if you're a Judeophile, you'll have to like me." Then he added, "I know two German women in Berlin you might want to interview. They recently converted to Judaism. They want to have children and raise them as Jews."

"It would be great to meet them, Professor Levin. I had two years of German in college."

"I don't think you'll need it with them—one of them for sure. And, by the way, please call me Adam." He wrote down the hotel where Clare would be staying—in case he could get her together with Zoe and Annika.

"Friends of yours?"

Adam hesitated. "I guess you could say that," he offered.

"And why are you going to Berlin, Adam?" she asked.

"It's very complicated," he replied.

"Oh," Clare said. She looked a little hurt. They had been communicating so openly.

"I'm sorry," he said. "Back at school, let's have dinner; I'll explain then. But I can't talk about it now. It's not you; I can't talk about it with anyone now."

"Spy stuff?" she said, intrigued.

"No, but equally hush-hush." Adam enjoyed the feeling of being on some kind of secret mission and that Clare seemed impressed. He noticed she had no wedding band or engagement ring on her finger, and this was a plus because he found everything about her charming.

"Well," she said, "I'll certainly be looking forward to that dinner. I…" she hesitated…"I had a boyfriend, but we broke up. I don't really know anyone at the university."

"Well," he said, "you do now."

Just then the plane hit some turbulence and bounced around in the air. Clare emitted a tiny scream and grabbed Adam's arm. "Oh, I'm sorry, Professor—uh, Adam. I didn't mean to do that." She looked frightened and embarrassed.

"Don't be sorry," Adam replied. "Do that whenever you'd like."

"Flying terrifies me."

In response, Adam lifted the arm rest between them. She smiled. And with that he took the liberty of lifting her hand and kissing it.

He had no idea how she might react, but her broadening smile was reassuring. She looked at him now with intensity, her face glowing. The plane hit another bump, and Clare again gripped Adam's arm. "You're absolutely sure you don't mind?"

"Quite the contrary," Adam said. "I'm hoping for more bumps. Do that anytime, frightened or not." Then he added, "I know this may seem sudden—maybe out of line. The plane is going to land soon but before it does, I'd really like to kiss you."

"Well," she said, leaning over the space between them, "don't expect any resistance from me."

CHAPTER 16

In the airport terminal Zoe was waiting for Adam at the carousel where his suitcase would soon appear. She rushed up to him, threw her arms around him, and kissed him firmly on the lips. Adam wanted her badly and felt sad he would soon be making love not to her but to a teacup.

He was aware that Clare was also waiting for her suitcase and had seen the passionate embrace and kiss. He imagined her thinking, "So this is the hush-hush thing you couldn't talk about?" She looked forlorn. He felt like rushing up to her and saying, "Look, this isn't what it looks like. I'm just over here as some kind of prize bull. I don't even get to mount the cows. It's as if they're extracting my sperm in a laboratory and injecting the cows with it. You and I are getting together when we're back in New Jersey. I'm really interested in you, really attracted to you."

While Zoe hugged and kissed him, part of him knew he was still in love with her and wished they were back at the Grand Canyon experiencing again those idyllic days and wished their embrace was exactly what it appeared to be.

Zoe's car, a gray Opel, was small by American standards—as were virtually all the cars in the parking lot.

"Gasoline," Zoe said, "costs almost five times what it costs in the United States, so Europeans drive small cars if they have cars at all."

Riding into town, Adam noticed that the most remarkable thing about West Berlin was there was nothing remarkable about it. It was a rather boring city architecturally. Flattened by allied bombing and shelling as the Americans and British from one side and the Russians from the other closed in on it in 1945, it had to be rebuilt in a hurry—and it showed. The housing was bland, the few public buildings were uninspired, and the store windows were dull. Adam thought he wouldn't be attracted to buying anything in those stores.

Zoe said there was little desire to restore the damaged old buildings that might have helped the city maintain some centuries-old charm. "People felt old buildings were reminiscent of fascism; they wanted to obliterate anything that might remind them of it. Modern buildings, even ugly ones, wiped the slate clean."

The predominant color of the city was gray. It looked like the 1950s. It had none of the charm of other European cities. It looked like a larger version of Kansas City. But many tri-color flags brightened the landscape. Zoe told him the flags were those of the Weimar Republic which preceded the Nazi rise to power and had now been revived.

Alongside the new but dull buildings were vacant lots full of rubble where nothing had been built or the occasional shell of a building that had yet to be demolished. Thirty years after the war, its effects could still be seen.

According to Zoe the dull look of the city was because it was not the capital. Bonn, far to the West, was the capital of West Germany. East Berlin was the capital of East Germany, and Zoe said it was even less attractive than West Berlin.

"Things may not look like much over here, but people are lively, funny. They can laugh at themselves. Compared to the other side of the wall, this is a party town. Annika and I don't get harassed because of our relationship. I don't think you could say the same yet about the United States. Most Wessies are reasonably accepting."

"Wessies?"

"West Berliners."

Then Zoe told Adam something surprising. "Even during the Nazi period, Berlin was a bit more liberal than other German cities. When Hitler wanted a rally or demonstration, he brought in trainloads of storm troopers from Munich. He got his lowest vote total in Berlin in 1933. This is where most of the Jews lived. It was also the intellectual and artistic center of Germany at the time. And it's beginning to become that way again."

Sure enough, as they turned a corner, Adam saw a young woman on the sidewalk wearing a T-shirt that said in English, "Sex Not Sects." It recalled for him the commune in California which had been about sex and sects. He held up his right thumb to the woman, not sure if she saw it or if Germans understood the gesture.

Getting closer to it, Adam could see the most interesting thing about the two Berlins: the wall that divided them like an unsightly scar. Here, more than anywhere else, the Iron Curtain had clanged down. Ah these Germans, Adam thought: their uncanny attraction to fencing people in. On the wall, every two hundred yards, there were watch towers, and Adam could see men in uniform up there with machine guns.

As they passed a curve in the wall, Adam could see an inner wall about fifty yards beyond the main wall. And just beyond it were apartment houses with most windows and doors facing West Berlin boarded up, some even bricked up. Zoe said the few that were not sealed were where members of the Communist party lived.

In between the two walls was a sand no-man's-land. "That's the death zone," Zoe said. "It's mined, and there are trip wires in it that set off flares. Some of the towers have automatic weapons that will instantly fire at a spot where someone has run into a wire in the sand—assuming a guard doesn't see them first and fire at them. Many have died trying to get to our side of the *Wall of Shame*, over one hundred already."

"Jeez," Adam said, "those Communists aren't kidding around."

Zoe said, "Some make it across the death zone and over the outer wall at night—but fewer since they put in the mines, trip wires, and automatic guns. They even have electric fences in the sewers, which East and West share. There are two hundred-sixty towers on the wall and nine hundred dogs. Ten thousand soldiers work shifts at the wall. Some escapees have tunneled to our side, digging from the basement of a building over there. A whole family and their friends—fifty-seven men, women, and children—made it before the tunnel was discovered and blown up. And there was a clever West Berliner who had legitimate business in East Berlin and managed to smuggle six people out, one by one, twisted like pretzels in the tiny front luggage compartment of his Volkswagen. The guards never thought to look there."

The watchtowers and wall further eroded Adam's belief that all Germans were equally evil.

The wall separated a better Germany from one that found freedom threatening. One totalitarianism had replaced another, Communists instead of Nazis.

But there was greater complexity for Adam to swallow. Zoe said, "There are people over there—not just Communists—who don't want the wall to come down. They have heard so much about how decadent we are over here that they don't want to be infected by us.

"In fact, some who escape are not happy here; they don't know what to do with themselves. The state controls everything in East Berlin. Now they're free and can't handle it; they keep to themselves and don't mix with us. That's also true of the few East Germans elsewhere who escape into bordering countries and then fly into West Berlin. They act like they're in a foreign country. One of them said to me, 'At least over there I knew where I stood. My apartment was not much grander than a large closet, but I could depend on that closet. I had a boring job, but at least I had a job. Here one is free—to starve.' The people who escape are like prisoners who get out of jail. They think maybe they should go back to jail. Here they have freedom but also responsibilities."

Zoe changed the subject but continued to undermine Adam's certitude about contemporary Germans. "Let's not forget that you Americans imported former Nazis to run your missile and space programs—people who should have gone to prison or even been hung. Werner von Braun, for example."

Thinking of the moral complexity of his own country bringing in Nazis to help America compete with the Russians again tore at the fabric of Adam's certainty that Germany had a monopoly on evil.

He also found himself thinking of the Berlin airlift of 1948–49 when West Berliners were seen in the West as victims, not villains. With the Russian blockade—an attempt to bring all of Berlin into the Soviet orbit—over two hundred thousand flights were made by the allies, bringing in food and other essentials; planes landed every forty-five seconds. And when the wall was built in 1961, it seemed to further make the people of West Berlin and West Germany in general admirable by comparison to East Berlin and East Germany. Adam found himself thinking that those who tried to escape from East Berlin deserved some recognition as…well, he wasn't yet comfortable referring to any Germans as heroes, though he could see why that might be how some might regard them.

He was also beginning to see why John Kennedy, when he came to West Berlin in 1963, said in a speech that if people wanted to understand the Cold War, "Let them come to Berlin." He then went on to say, "All free men, wherever they may live, are citizens of Berlin, and therefore, as a free man, I take pride in the words"—and here Kennedy made his historic remark in German—"*Ich bin ein Berliner*" (I am a Berliner) to wild applause and cheering.

Thinking of Kennedy's speech chipped away further at Adam's resolve to have nothing to do with Germany or Germans with the exception of Zoe and, he supposed, Annika—though he reserved judgement on the latter for the present. Kennedy had made his famous remark twelve years before, after the wall had been up for two years. Adam was in Berlin for a far more intimate purpose than what had brought Kennedy here. Whether he liked it or not, wasn't he, in some sense, about to become a Berliner too, to join a once hated society and culture?

Whatever he once felt, Berlin and especially its wall preoccupied Adam. He asked Zoe whether she thought it would ever come down.

"Someday, perhaps" she said. "It will be difficult because we in West Berlin live on an island—an island not surrounded by water. There is a popular song, 'Der Insulaner verliert die Ruhe nicht.' It means 'The islander doesn't lose patience.' We West Berliners are islanders in two ways: the wall, but also because Berlin is deep inside East Germany. And if the wall ever does come down, there will still be the wall in our minds. That one will take time."

"What do you mean by the wall in our minds?"

"We've grown used to the separation. Even if the wall comes down, it may take years before we again think of Berlin as one city. Also, will its two parts fuse together—

all of the arteries and tendons and ligaments and nerves reconnect? The Communism of East Berlin is probably the most extreme in the Soviet bloc because it is separated only by a wall from Western values."

As they drove along, Adam asked Zoe to explain a large mound of dirt he could see in the distance.

"They say the Führerbunker is under there. That's where Hitler was when the Russians were closing in. He married Eva Braun there, then they killed themselves, and their bodies were burned in a ditch just outside the bunker. The Russians dynamited part of it, but most of it is supposed to still be under there."

"Why haven't they excavated it?" Adam asked. "The history?"

"It might be a rallying place for neo-Nazis. They may build a parking lot over it."

"You still have Nazis?" Adam said with fervor.

"A few," she said, "but doesn't everyone—probably more in the United States than here. You Americans think that anyone can believe whatever they want, and I respect that, but we Germans can't afford that luxury when it comes to Nazis."

Zoe turned her car down a street which ran for one long block, reaching almost to the wall. She stopped part way. "I want to show you something," she said. They got out of the car, and Adam followed her into a large, rubble filled lot that was, as Adam later learned, immediately behind her building. Part of the lot had been cleared of chunks of concrete and bricks that were everywhere else, and there was a little garden, some of it planted under cold frames like little green houses where, even at this early date, lettuce, beets, and other vegetables grew. He helped Zoe pick some. "This will be our salad tonight," she said.

Adam told her of the victory garden he had as a child during World War II.

"Well," said Zoe, "the last thing today's Germans want is victory. Many of us are pacifists. Annika and I call this our peace garden."

They got back in the car, and Zoe said, "This is our street, Schneiderstrasse." She told him that *schneider* meant "tailor," *strasse*, "street." She added that the street had once been occupied by a number of Jewish tailors and their shops. Adam remembered Mrs. Schneiderman, the neighbor who had been happy to take his radishes. He supposed a literal translation of Schneiderman would be "tailor man." Zoe continued, "Neither Annika nor I can even sew on a button, and we are the only Jews on the street now," she said.

"Welcome to the tribe."

"Shalom" she said.

"You probably know a great deal more about Judaism than I do."

"Not to worry, Adam. We'll make a good Jew out of you too," she said with a laugh.

They continued down the street to the end. Sitting on the front stoop of Schneiderstrasse 41 was a young woman who could only be Annika. She was reading a magazine but dropped it and rose as Zoe parked her car at the curb. She was just as in the pictures and moved with a catlike grace. She was more beautiful than her pictures; she was dark where Zoe was fair. Zoe had told Adam that Annika was a model while attending law school. She wore jeans and a sweatshirt with three sayings written across it in English.

Shit happens. [Taoist Proverb]
Shit happens because you are bad. [Catholic Proverb]
Why does this shit keep happening to us? [Jewish Proverb]

Adam pointed to the sweatshirt and laughed. These women were absolutely serious about being Jews. And the funny sweatshirt immediately broke the ice with Annika, but he didn't know how to greet her, a woman with whom he was presumably going to father a child. Should he shake hands, kiss her on the cheek, what?

Annika decided for him. She reached out, threw her arms around him, and then kissed him on both cheeks in the European fashion.

"My turn," Adam said, kissing her on both cheeks too.

That didn't seem to be enough. Annika then kissed him on the lips as Zoe had in the airport, while Zoe looked on beaming. Adam wondered, why did Zoe and Annika kiss him with such passion? Could they afford to do so because it was understood this was as far as it would go, so why not? Adam had never before been kissed on the lips by a woman that wasn't part of what hopefully was to come next?

"You ladies in heat?" Adam asked with a smile.

Annika panted loudly, and Adam laughed. "Did you bring the sperm?" she asked. She, like Zoe, spoke nearly flawless English, but with a somewhat more noticeable accent.

"Yeah," Adam said, laughing, "I've got it safely packed away. Got the eggs?"

"We think so," Zoe said.

"Well then," Adam said with a smile, "we'll have to introduce them to each other."

Both women collapsed with laughter, and Adam joined them. He was embarking on a strange love affair with these two women, simultaneously nonsexual and intensely sexual—making babies was certainly sexual. Presumably, that was what sex was for. He still favored Zoe, but he was less completely stuck on her. Clare on the plane had chipped away at his exclusive attachment, and Annika was eroding it further. He especially liked that she made him laugh. It was going to be all right.

"Okay," Adam said, "take me upstairs and introduce me to that gorgeous teacup. I can't wait to meet her."

CHAPTER 17

Zoe and Annika wanted to carry Adam's suitcase upstairs. "That's okay," he said. "I've got it."

"We want to take care of you," Annika said. "Pamper you, I think is how you say it in America. Our apartment is two flights up. No elevator."

"That's okay," Adam said. "Heavy objects build muscle. I'm going to need a strong right arm for this baby making business."

"You'll do it right-handed?" she asked with a laugh. She squeezed Adam's right bicep, nodded in approval, and everyone laughed. He was starting to like Annika more and more. She was bolder than Zoe, funnier. She had more of an edge, but he liked that edge.

"And should we presume you would prefer night to daytime?"

"Oh, yes, night," Adam replied. "More romantic. And, besides, I get sleepy after sex."

"Well," Annika continued in her jocular way, "you go to work tomorrow night. Tonight, you catch up on your sleep and get over the jet lag."

Zoe opened the apartment door. She asked if Adam minded taking off his shoes; both women were taking off theirs and placing them in a bin by the door. Adam said he liked the idea, had been to Asia several times and noticed people in places like Japan and Korea would never dream of walking into their homes, or anyone else's, with their shoes on. They took them off and walked in their stocking feet or put on shoes or slippers reserved for indoors. "We Americans are barbarians," Adam said. "We wear the same shoes indoors and out and carry into our homes all manner of shit, so we are forever cleaning our houses or, if wealthy enough, hiring others to clean them. We think we're civilized, but in this we're barbarians." He vowed to himself that he would change his own habits when returning to the United States and insist that those entering his home remove their shoes as well, offended or not.

Zoe led Adam down the hall. "This is your room," she said. "It will be the nursery." She didn't have to say that the bedroom he had caught a glimpse of as they passed— the big one with the queen-sized bed and white duvet— was theirs. It was one thing to think of such a bed in the abstract, quite another to actually see it. Adam felt pain in seeing the bed and wished it was his and Zoe's.

Nevertheless, his own room was well lit and pleasant: a single bed with a green corduroy bedspread, a desk and chair, an electric typewriter on the desk, and a large bookcase full of English language books, including several Adam had always meant to read and others favorites from the past. Two of his own books were there too. "Nice room," he told the women. Zoe said, "We wanted you to have a typewriter. We borrowed this one from the office. We'd be honored by anything you might write while here."

His window faced the wall. He could look out any-time at the central fact of Berlin life: the wall. There was graffiti on the West Berlin side of the main wall—mostly in German but some in English or partly in English. One, painted in red, inside a huge heart, said "Heinz and Helga." Such messages gave the wall a ca-sual look, as if it wasn't to be overly concerned about. Adam wondered whether Heinz and Helga were still lovers. Otherwise, it would be like an outdated tat-too inked on one's body, an embarrassing celebration of a relationship that no longer existed. Another piece of graffiti, completely in English said, "FUCK THE WALL." Amen to that, Adam thought. The wall took a long curve beginning shortly beyond Adam's window. Further along on the curve he lost sight of the outside of the main wall but could see its inside. It was painted white and completely free of graffiti. Obviously, anyone racing towards the wall from East Berlin had no time for graffiti; their only concern was getting over the wall alive.

Shortly after the curve began, there was a tower. It had a flag atop it that looked just like the West German flags he had seen driving into town, but there was an insignia in the middle of it. Adam could make out a soldier in the tower who seemed to be looking right at him with large black binoculars. Below him, about one hundred yards further on, another soldier was raking the sand smooth. Annika said a young man had made it over the wall there the day before; it was in the newspapers. The footprints in the sand were, no doubt, an embarrassment.

Zoe asked Adam if he wanted to freshen up before dinner. "There's hot water," she said. Indeed, he did crave a shower to wash the trip off. The bathroom was between the two bedrooms and was the only one, so Adam would be sharing it with the women. Its blue and white tiles gave it a homey look. It would be in the bathroom, he supposed, where he would produce his baby making contributions.

The shower was different from what Adam was used to. There was a small electrically heated water tank on the bathroom wall, and one had to fire it up at least half an hour in advance. Annika had already done this while Zoe was fetching him from the airport. The shower head wasn't attached to the wall. It was on a flexible plastic hose, and you held it in your hand and sprayed yourself. Given the size of the water tank, Adam decided it was best to wet himself, turn off the water while he soaped up, and then turn it on again to rinse off. It would use less hot water. Europeans, in Adam's experience, were more attentive to limiting energy use than Americans. One didn't take long showers in Europe.

While Zoe made dinner, Adam looked down out the back window on the rubble filled lot and tiny vegetable garden behind the building and then joined Annika who sat on the couch in the living room. "Tell me about yourself, Annika. I know something about Zoe's origins, but not about yours."

"Well," she said, "I was born the same year as Zoe, 1945. Unlike her, I had a father. He never talked about it, but I learned from my mother, after they got a divorce, that he had been a Nazi—S.S. no less, a Jew killer. He would have killed people like you and people like Zoe and me as well—although, for the Nazis, being a Jew was racial. If a Jew converted to Christianity, they killed you anyway. I doubt anyone converted to Judaism in those days. I wonder if the Nazis, with their racial theories, would have killed converts for being Jews or for being mentally deficient. Anyone would have been crazy to convert to Judaism then.

"I broke off relations with my father years ago when I found out about him. I meet my mother for lunch once a month. My sister doesn't approve of lesbians, so there's only my mother that I see regularly."

"What does your mother think about your converting to Judaism?"

"I was raised Catholic, but I gave that up by high school. My mother still goes to church and is glad I have some religion now, no matter what it is. She was close friends with her Jewish neighbors before the war. She woke up one day, and they were no longer there. I suppose they ended up in Dachau or Buchenwald. Most of the German Jews ended up in death camps on German soil."

"And how does your mother feel about Zoe, Zoe and you?"

"She doesn't really understand it, but she wants grandchildren and is thrilled that I may have a child soon. I haven't told her just how—not sure she would approve."

"And what does Zoe's mother know?"

"Oh, she knows everything. Zoe talks to her on the phone at least once a week. She's coming to visit us next month. She's excited about possibly being a grandmother too."

"I feel like I'm about to have two mothers-in-law."

"It is a little like that," Annika admitted, smiling. "Zoe's mother says she would like to meet you some day."

"Well, good thing she's not coming now. I'm not sure I could handle that," Adam said feeling a bit ashamed for what the woman had endured at the age of sixteen.

Zoe called them in to dinner. There was going to be chicken and salad from that blossoming ruin of a backyard.

The apartment had no dining room, but the round oak table and matching chairs in the kitchen were more than adequate. "It's nice to have a man here for Shabbat," Zoe said, using the Hebrew word for the sabbath.

Adam had not realized it was Friday evening. Where'd you get the challah?" he asked. The table was set with candles, wine, and a braided challah bread.

"From the Jewish bakery," Annika replied. "Everyone goes there, not just the few Jews. It's the best bakery in Berlin. They also make bagels, really good ones."

That was another nail in the coffin of Uncle Jack's hatred of Germany and Germans. How could he fully hate a place that had a fine Jewish bakery?

Zoe and Annika lit the candles together, reciting the prayer in Hebrew. "Now you," Annika said, "the prayer on the wine. Somehow that's a man's prayer." Adam hadn't recited it or any other prayer for years, but, albeit rusty, he managed it with a little help from the women. Then the three of them together recited the prayer on the challah.

Adam was strangely moved. Tears welled up in his eyes. "What's the matter, Adam? Zoe asked.

"Nothing," Adam said. "Here I am in Berlin, Germany celebrating the Jewish sabbath with two German women who have become Jews. I'm crying not out of sadness but of joy."

"*Am Yisrael chai,*" Annika said. "The people Israel lives."

After dinner Annika washed the dishes. Zoe took down a fine porcelain teacup with roses on it from the cupboard. "Teacup," she said, "this is Adam. Adam this is Teacup."

"Pleased to meet you, Teacup," Adam said. "What are your thoughts about sex on the first date?" He began to whistle an old American song.

"What song is that?" Zoe asked.

"'Tea for Two,'" Adam replied.

Zoe roared with laughter. Annika at the sink joined in the merriment.

After dinner they watched a movie together on the living room couch. Adam wasn't sure how to sit. Maybe Zoe and Annika wanted to sit together. But, no, they insisted he sit between them. As had been the case his first night at the Grand Canyon with Zoe, he didn't know what to do with his arms. He kept his hands in his lap. Annika took his arm and pulled it around her. There was something delightfully forward about her. Feminine but direct. He put the other one around Zoe.

Both women snuggled against him. Was he their father, husband, boyfriend, or son? Maybe a little of each.

What an ego trip, Adam thought. Two beautiful women wanted to have his babies. How many men ever received such invitations?

After the movie Adam went to bed to catch up on his rest and get on the German clock. At some point in the night, he dreamed he was atop a mountain and countless women were scaling the heights to reach him, the only man on the planet with sperm. The rest of the men had been sterilized by radiation from some kind of nuclear attack. But there were so many women after him—an entire planet of them. There were no Nazis in this dream. It seemed as if his dreams and his life were coming into closer conformity to one another.

The next day, after breakfast, Annika took Adam for a long walk in West Berlin. Being Saturday, she had the day off; Zoe was the duty lawyer at their law firm. He suspected the women had arranged things this way, so he and Annika could get to know each other better, which was fine with him.

First Annika took him by the Jewish bakery, and they bought some bagels for the next day's breakfast. They also bought a small tub of cream cheese with bits of smoked salmon folded into it for their toasted bagels.

Adam wanted to see as much of the wall as possible, marveling at how much effort and expense the East German authorities had put into imprisoning their people. Annika took him down the street called Friedrichstrasse to one of the few openings in the wall, Checkpoint Charlie, where demonstrations of West Berliners took place on a regular basis, hoping to inspire East Berliners to rise up against their oppressors. West Berliners could occasionally get papers to go into East Berlin at Checkpoint Charlie—if they had important business or wished to make major purchases helpful to the East Berlin economy.

Annika said, "The man Zoe was briefly married to went through Checkpoint Charlie after their divorce and never came back. We learned he was greeted as a hero by the authorities over there but then wanted to come back and couldn't. No East Berliner can come our way without being shot at."

Adam noticed the large sign at Checkpoint Charlie: YOU ARE LEAVING THE AMERICAN SECTOR repeated in smaller letters in Russian, French, and German. "This is where the tank standoff took place, in 1961, right?" Adam asked. The American M-48s and the Russian T-55s. Sixteen hours pointing at each other with their cannons; luckily, nobody fired."

"I don't pay any attention to politics," Annika said "How come you know? You just arrived."

"I did a lot reading," Adam replied.

"But Zoe told me you wanted nothing to do with Germany, hated everything about it, past, present, and future."

"I did. But you women are changing things for me or, at least, complicating them. It's your fault," he said with a smile.

Annika laughed. She took Adam down to the Spree River where there was no wall; the river itself was the barrier. Apparently, East Berlin considered the entire river to be theirs, right to the West Berlin bank. Across the river Adam could see armed guards patrolling. Annika said that two escapees had drowned trying to cross the river, and others had been shot dead in the water, their bodies left to float away. If anyone from West Berlin went into the water to retrieve a body, they were shot at. The guards wanted the body to float along as an example to others thinking of escaping across the river. She also told him if anyone on the west bank fell into the river, they could not be rescued by others; they had entered East Berlin without permission. Recently, she said, an eight-year-old boy chasing a ball as it bounced down the embankment, slid on the mud into the river and drowned. Older children were there who might have saved him, but they had been instructed by their parents never to go into the river or even close to the bank. They had to watch that boy drown, and the soldiers on the other bank did nothing.

Annika took Adam to lunch at a festive café in the Tiergarten, Berlin's Central Park, where a rock band of teenagers was playing—mostly Beatles songs. They were certainly noisy enough. Adam couldn't help thinking how closely they resembled hopeful garage bands in the United States. He wondered whether they knew any English besides what was in the songs and whether they actually understood the words or could just imitate the sounds.

Annika recommended the bratwurst sausage, which by comparison made American hot dogs, Adam thought, taste like plastic—with the possible exception of Hebrew National. He felt a certain pride that Jews made the best

American hot dog. Then he thought of his discomfort at eating a frankfurter in the airport and how his more unreasonable hatred of all things German was continuing to dissipate. Even people speaking German no longer sounded so harsh; increasingly it was just another language he didn't know.

Restoration of the Tiergarden's war damage was still going on. Many of its statues had been knocked over or smashed by allied bombs, and most of its trees destroyed from the air as well or cut down by freezing Berliners seeking firewood because there was no coal. Most of the park was already returned to its former beauty with a wealth of spring flowers up and ready to bloom—tulips, daffodils, hyacinths. Adam felt a certain comfort seeing these familiar flowers.

When they left the park, Annika insisted they take a cab back to the apartment. Adam would have preferred to walk, but Annika said, "We've walked over half of West Berlin, and I don't want to exhaust you. You have an important mission tonight."

"Okay, boss," Adam said.

That evening Annika made dinner and Zoe, who had returned from work, chatted with Adam on the couch. At the table Adam said, "Meat? We had it at lunch and now again. Somehow, not sure why, I thought you would be a vegetarian, Annika, that it fit your personality."

"I was. But then I learned Hitler had been a vegetarian, so I gave it up. Today's Germans do our best not to be like him in any way—though maybe we overdo it."

"Besides being a vegetarian, he loved dogs and kissed babies," Adam said. "Horrible to say, but he was human."

"Yes," she replied. "How I wish he hadn't been. How much easier if he had simply been a monster, with long canine teeth and blood running down his chin. A vampire, a zombie. But, no, he was human. Hopefully, that doesn't mean there's a little of Hitler in all of us."

"I suspect there is," Adam replied and felt better about himself for having said it. The black and white world of his youth continued to dissipate.

After dinner it was time for Adam to go to work. The women had a few pornographic magazines available, but he said he didn't want them. "I have nothing against pornography," he said, "but it's boring, no story." He went into the bathroom with the teacup.

CHAPTER 18

Masturbation was not something Adam had done much of since coming of age. He still did it from time to time, but it always left him a little sad and lonely. He had no moral compunctions against it; sex with a partner was simply much more interesting, more fulfilling. It had a story behind it

He had never before, except once, had trouble masturbating, but he was having trouble now. The other time was when he and his wife were being checked for fertility. Now, as then, he felt no desire, no lust; it was simply mechanical. It reminded him of what that young hitchhiker had told him out West about disliking the word blow job because of the job part of it. What he was doing now was definitely a job! Ah, for a premature ejaculation, he told himself. Where's a premature ejaculation when you could use one? After about fifteen minutes, Zoe knocked on the bathroom door and said, "Are you all right, Adam?"

"Fine," he answered, though he definitely was not fine. And he was more than a little embarrassed. It was like anything sexual: if you tried hard, it didn't happen. Perhaps he should have brought those pornographic magazines into the bathroom with him after all.

It was taking a long time to get erect, and he wondered as he stared into the bathroom mirror what the problem was. Perhaps it was doing it with his right hand while holding the teacup in his left, ready, waiting, expectant. Also, maybe he was afraid he would drop it, as he had dropped his wife's mustache cup in that dreary Indiana hotel dream. He put the teacup down on the sink.

He needed a sexual fantasy. He thought of how it had been with Zoe at the Grand Canyon, but it didn't help because she was nearby in the apartment. Thoughts of Annika's lean, willowy form crept into his mind, and it helped because of the novelty of imagining sex with her. He did feel a bit guilty, but it was silly given their present relationship.

At last, he was erect and after what seemed like a very long time, with his penis sore, he reached for the teacup and managed to ejaculate into it.

He put down the cup, zipped up his fly, and emerged from the bathroom holding the cup in an elegant fashion, his pinky pointing up as if he was at high tea in England. "Okay, ladies," he said with a smile, "get it while it's hot."

Zoe and Annika thanked him and went into their room, one carrying the teacup, the other the turkey baster. They were in there a long time. Adam sat on the couch watching television and wondering exactly what they were doing in there. Were they simply inserting his semen or were they making love as part of their reproduction plan? An hour went by. Adam felt lonely, excluded, left out.

Finally, he went to his room, got into bed, and selected Hemingway's *A Farewell to Arms* from the bookshelf to read again. He wondered: had he chosen this book out of anger, some sort of passive aggression—knowing that Lieutenant Henry's love, Catherine, would die in childbirth at the end of the book?

In the morning Zoe, who would be spending the day with him, said, "You look a little glum. Everything all right?"

"Fine," Adam said, then admitted, "I felt a little abandoned last night. Kinda lonesome. Jerking off isn't sexy for me, and then you two went off by yourselves and the affection I was feeling for both of you went south."

"South?'"

"Diminished."

"We'll have to fix that tonight," she said. "We don't just want your sperm; we want you to be part of this, emotionally as much as physically. I'll talk to Annika."

Zoe took Adam aboard the U-Bahn subway. It was rather cheerful in contrast to the subways in New York City; the trains were smooth and quiet, and the entrance and platform were clean of litter. Zoe had a monthly pass good for both of them, but there was no one to show it to. There were no turnstiles; you just walked onto the platform. "Do people ever cheat?" he asked Zoe.

"A few, perhaps."

Adam found it remarkable that the subway was on the honor system. Germany and the Germans continued to surprise him. The most rigidly authoritarian people had now become the most liberal, the most civilized—the

West Berliners anyway. Quite despite himself, Adam was increasingly finding reasons to like Germans.

He asked if the subway kept going into East Berlin.

"It does," Zoe said, "but we West Berliners have to get off at the last stop on our side of the wall, unless we have special papers. Otherwise, we'll be arrested. East Berliners exit at the last stop on their side. You could probably keep going into East Berlin with your American passport. They often let tourists in."

Adam and Zoe exited the U-Bahn in the Bavarian Quarter portion of the Schöneberg District. Zoe said this had been largely a Jewish neighborhood. Sixteen thousand Jews had lived here and virtually all were rounded up and "concentrated," five families to an apartment. Then, one night they were removed and sent to the death camps. Among the Jews who escaped were Nelly Sachs, who, in Sweden, won the Nobel Prize for Literature and Billy Wilder, the film director, who made his way to France and then to Hollywood.

An area of the district had been developed by the builder, Georg Haberland, and the key street was named for him, Haberlandstrasse. The Nazis had changed its name; they wouldn't have a street named after a Jew, but now it was back with its original name. Albert Einstein had lived on this street for fifteen years. His house, number five, had been destroyed during the war and the house replacing it was number eight, but there was a plaque on it honoring Einstein.

Zoe showed Adam a memorial on Munich Street where a synagogue had stood dating from 1909. "It was burned during Kristalnacht," she said. "That was when Jews learned there was no future for them in Germany, and the smart ones tried to get out. But too many of them were strong German patriots and had fought heroically in World War I. They couldn't bring themselves to leave, so they ended up in the death camps." Adam learned that the remains of the synagogue were taken down in 1956 because there were no Jews to worship there.

But there was a plan afoot to someday build a Jewish museum nearby and to put up a large Holocaust memorial elsewhere in the city. "Isn't it interesting how we human beings celebrate those we've murdered or mistreated," Adam said. "It's what we Americans do with the Indians; a museum is being planned in Washington. It's better than nothing, but it would be still better if there were no compelling reason to build it."

Zoe said that one of the neighborhoods in the Shoneberg District, surrounding the Nollendorfplatz (Adam had learned that "platz" meant plaza or square), had been the center of gay life in Berlin during the Weimar Republic prior to the ascent of the Nazis to power. The gay British writer Christopher Isherwood had lived there, and his book, *Goodbye to Berlin* was inspired by it. The area was also the inspiration for the stage musical and movie, *Cabaret*.

That night Adam went to work again in the bathroom. And it was work. He did a little better this time; he was getting the hang of it. When he had ejaculated and handed the cup over to the women, they asked him if he would like to be with them.

"Gee, I don't know," Adam said. "Two's company; three's a crowd. Besides, won't that be embarrassing for you?"

"Not for us, maybe for you?" Annika said.

"Not in the slightest," Adam said. It wasn't the whole truth, but he was curious.

The three went into the women's dimly lit bedroom. "Where do I go?" Adam asked.

"Between us," Zoe said.

Adam climbed onto the bed and lay down in the middle. He wondered how they would proceed.

Both women were wearing loose fitting nightgowns. They took off their underpants and lay down beside him. "You should go first," Annika said to Zoe. "I went first last night but save half of it for me."

Zoe joked, "Like the half you left me last night?"

Adam was concerned he wasn't producing enough to go around. But there were millions of the little guys in each ejaculation, and it only took one. Annika put her arms around him and kissed him on the neck. "We love you Adam," she said.

He watched as Zoe, sitting up, lubricated the turkey baster with what he assumed was petroleum jelly. She inserted the end of it into the teacup, pressed the rubber bulb, and then slid the baster into her body.

Now it was Annika's turn. "You don't have any venereal diseases, do you Zoe?" she asked with a laugh.

"Not unless I caught one from you," Zoe joked back.

"Hey, there's hardly any left in here," Annika said. "Don't be so greedy next time."

"Quit complaining. I left half," Zoe said.

"I'll tell you, ladies," Adam said, "there's nothing quite the equal of having two women fighting over one's sperm. Tomorrow night I'll try to give you a bucket full."

Annika followed the same procedure as Zoe, and meanwhile, Zoe hugged Adam and kissed him on his forehead and cheeks. "We love you, Adam," she also said.

"Hey," Annika called. "Take it easy. This isn't the Grand Canyon." Adam was relieved when both women laughed. It definitely wasn't the Grand Canyon, and everyone knew it. Someday, perhaps, he would be able to joke about the Grand Canyon too.

When Annika had finished, both women hugged and kissed Adam from either side of him. "We love you," Annika repeated.

"And I both of you," he said. He wasn't sure that was quite true of Annika yet, but saying it made it more so.

"You are no longer married to Hitler, Adam," Zoe said. "You're married to us."

"Good deal," Adam said. "You're both better looking."

He made an effort to get up and head for his room, thinking that was what the two women would expect him to do, but they wouldn't let go of him and insisted he stay with them. He slipped off his clothes and lay down between them in just his underpants. Eventually, all three fell asleep.

"Adam!" Zoe whispered, gently shaking him. "Time to get up."

"What?" He had been dreaming. He couldn't remember anything about the dream, just how it had felt. Warm, he thought. Nothing like that terrible dream he had in Indiana—his by now ex-wife with the Hitler mustache.

Light was streaming through the venetian blinds; a new day had begun. Annika too was slowly coming awake. She yawned and said, "I hope we've fulfilled a favorite male fantasy for you, Adam: sleeping with two women at the same time."

"Sorry, but that's never been a fantasy of mine. Besides, sleeping with implies having sex, and we're not doing that."

"True," Annika said, "but I bet you wouldn't mind doing exactly that with each of us, you pervert you."

"Probably true, "Adam said, "but one at a time."

Actually, this was no longer where his mind was. His single-minded attachment to Zoe continued to erode as his affection for Annika grew. He had begun to think of both women as his best friends, not lovers or potential lovers, perhaps even more like his sisters. It was Clare who increasingly occupied his thoughts. The intimacy on the plane. Their kiss.

"Enough talk," Zoe said. "Let's have breakfast."

After breakfast, Zoe did the dishes. Adam noticed the care with which she washed the teacup and placed it in the drain tray. "I'm not putting it into the dish washer," she said. "I don't want to chance it hitting against something and cracking."

"Well, if it does you must have others, don't you?" Adam asked.

"Yes, but this one is sacred now," Zoe replied. "When it's served its purpose, we'll have to enshrine it in some way. The most venerated object in our private museum."

She also washed the turkey baster with great care.

Both women needed to go to work that day, so Adam decided to experience West Berlin on his own. He would hike along the wall. Annika said, "Be careful. There are strange people in Berlin as in any city, and you know virtually no German. If you meet someone, and they speak no English, just say "Amerikaner."

Adam thanked her and said, "I'll get along. I'm picking up words here and there. For example, the wall: Die Mauer." He increasingly was no longer finding the German language ugly and oppressive. It was becoming just like any other foreign language, and he was eager to learn more of it. "See you tonight," he said. "Don't worry—I'll report for duty on time."

CHAPTER 19

It was a beautiful spring day, and the buds on the cherry trees were ready to burst into bloom. Adam walked down to the end of Schneiderstrasse and turned left on the narrow, cobblestone street that ran there under the wall. He was determined to see as much of the wall as he could. It would be a project to occupy his mind and provide some exercise. He was also looking forward to adventuring in Berlin alone, not under the protection of Zoe or Annika.

He soon came across a huge piece of graffiti. Painted on the wall top to bottom in rainbow colors was simply the English word "WHY?" The street continued for what he reckoned to be a mile and then was blocked by an apartment building built against the wall. He turned left, heading away from the wall, then turned right, and looked for a street that would get him back to the wall—not one that dead ended there but where there was an alley or street allowing him to continue along it as before.

The first street didn't work, nor the second. The third also ended at the wall, but to the left there was a dusty alley that soon widened and became a street wide enough for cars to be parked on it. There was even a bench on the sidewalk where he sat and rested for a while. He noticed for the first time the rubble stacked up against the wall at intervals. Must be for people who want to look over the wall he imagined.

He thought of Clare and his promise to call her and introduce her to the two German women who had converted to Judaism. But, of course, those two German women were Zoe and Annika, and things were already complicated; he didn't think he could handle adding Clare to the mix. He also didn't want her to know just what he was up to with Zoe and Annika. Not now. That might jeopardize a possible future with her. He wanted a chance to tell her the whole story from the beginning, not have her catch it in bits and pieces. Despite what she had seen in the airport, it was, he thought, safer in the long run not to call.

Rested, he got up from the bench and continued on. Luckily, he couldn't get lost; on the way back, he just had to somehow follow the wall back to Schneiderstrasse. All along the route he saw graffiti, but now he saw something that stunned him. It was a large swastika. Was it applied in hatred of Germany's all but non-existent Jews? Or was it expressing something else: hatred of the Communists on the other side of the wall? Or both?

Adam looked up and was surprised to see a watchtower just above him. A window was open, and the guard was looking down at him. He was momentarily frightened. "Amerikaner," Adam said.

The guard nodded. "I like speak English," he said.

"Tell me," Adam said, "How is it guarding this tower?"

"Boring you say, no?" the guard said. "I no shoot nobody. You see Swastika?"

"I do," Adam said.

"No Nazis our side wall. We kill all. Your side, some still walk around."

He had a point. Adam remembered in his reading that Konrad Adenauer, leader of West Germany after the war, had once said, in defending the presence of some low-ranking ex-Nazis or Nazi sympathizers working in his government, that he needed their managerial experience. "Dirty water," he said, "is better than no water at all."

Also, West Germany was a democracy, so justice proceeded slowly. Wasn't thirty years enough? Adam didn't think it worthwhile to converse with the guard about how the niceties of judicial procedures precluded the West German democracy from expeditiously hunting down, trying, executing or jailing every former Nazi, even if it removed from circulation a considerable portion of the population—though before meeting Zoe he would have argued for precisely that. Now, he had to admit, graffiti on his side of the wall—even the occasional Swastika—might be the price of free expression.

Just then, something struck the window alongside the guard's head. It made a ping noise. Adam turned and saw a youth in a nearby apartment house who had fired a BB gun at the guard. Adam wondered whether the guard would fire at the boy. The guard pointed his rifle but didn't fire. "Bad boy," he said to Adam. He closed the window and turned away.

Adam continued his expedition along the wall. Some of the graffiti was protest art: there was a crude rendition of Picasso's *Guernica*, the ultimate protest painting.

Copies of other famous paintings had no political significance. There were crude versions of Goya's *La Maja Desnuda* and Matisse's *L'Atelier Rouge* on the wall, both favorites of Adam's. This part of the wall seemed to be for artists learning their trade. They had at their disposal the longest "canvas" in the world.

Adam realized that if the wall ever came down all this art would be sacrificed. Also, he wasn't sure he wanted the wall to come down. It would come down when both parts of the city, East and West Germany as well, were unified. A unified Germany could become a menace all over again.

There was a street vendor near the paintings who was cooking and selling Bratwurst sandwiches, and Adam bought one and a Coca-Cola. He sat on a flat boulder up against the wall to have his lunch. He felt wonderfully free of cares and realized how much he was enjoying this day exploring on his own.

Continuing along the wall, he came upon a chubby man with a beard who sported a beret. Probably a Frenchman, Adam thought. The man was busy painting not on the wall but on a canvas placed on an easel next to the wall. There was something familiar about the picture's style. Adam sat on a bench and watched the man paint. He turned and, wiping his brush on a rag while looking at Adam, said something in German Adam recognized, *"Sprechen Sie Deutsch?"*

"Nein," Adam said. "Amerikaner." The man laughed. He was American too.

Adam was surprised. "What are you doing here?"

"I live here," the man said. "Was in Berlin during the war. Army. Met a German woman, and after I got out of the army, came back and married her. They say the Russians raped two million women after entering Germany; we Americans, for the most part, had love affairs. But tell me: what are you doing here?

"Visiting friends."

"Who?"

"Zoe Hildebrandt and Annika…" he realized he didn't know Annika's last name.

"Zoe and Annika?! I can't believe it. They're good friends of mine and my wife's. Bought one of my pictures."

"I thought I saw a painting in their apartment in your style."

"Yes, that's mine. Lesbians, you know."

"I know."

"Both gorgeous."

"Some of the handsomest men are gay, so things even out. Imagine the competition for women if those gorgeous guys weren't gay. The rest of us would be put out of business."

The painter wanted to know why Adam was staying with the women. "Ah," Adam said "that I can't tell you, but I suspect you'll find out eventually. Tell me," he continued, "how come you paint here by the wall? Don't you have a studio?"

"I do," the man said, "but on nice days I paint by the wall. Berlin is like Siamese twins who won't talk to each other. Being where the twins are joined—this wall—inspires me. In the morning it provides shade. But, mostly, it gives me ideas. I stare at it and ideas jump into my head—usually having nothing to do with the wall."

Adam noticed that the current painting was a seascape with fishing boats. "By the way," he said, "my name is Adam Levin."

"Jewish?"

Adam nodded. "Me too," the man said and stuck out his hand. "Bob Davis. Everybody loves Jews now in Berlin. They want to make up for the Holocaust, but, of course, they can't. Some even convert to Judaism—Zoe and Annika, for example. I hear they even want to have children and raise them as Jews."

"That's correct," Adam said.

"I doubt they'll look Jewish," Davis said.

"Hardly anyone looks Jewish anymore," Adam replied, laughing. "We've been mixing with people around the world for two thousand years. There's very little Semite left in us. Anti-Semitism is a dumb word. The Arabs, among the most virulent anti-Semites in the world, are actually the Semites."

"You've got a point," Davis said, turning back to his painting. Then he called over his shoulder, "Give my regards to Zoe and Annika."

Adam decided it was time to turn around and head back to Schneiderstrasse. Nearing the apartment, he saw a bald, familiar figure walking towards him dressed in a suit and carrying a briefcase. It was Rick Baum from the German Department of New Jersey University. Adam wondered what he was doing here; then he remembered reading in the faculty newsletter that Baum had a Fulbright lectureship at the Free University of Berlin this semester.

Adam had often wondered why a Jew would choose to teach German or even want to learn it. But here he was in Berlin learning a bit of it himself and running into or hearing of Jews everywhere—Davis the painter, now Baum, Annika and Zoe converting, and their American rabbi. Jews were popping up like spring flowers—as if miraculously emerging from mass graves.

"Small world," Baum said sticking out his hand when he spotted Adam. He was on his way to deliver a lecture on the American-oriented movies of the German filmmakers, Wim Wenders and Werner Herzog. Adam had reluctantly acknowledged, in recent years, that Wenders and Herzog were great filmmakers, German or not.

CHAPTER 20

A dam got back to the apartment in time for dinner and his nightly duties. At dinner Annika asked if he would like to join them in bed later.

"That's okay," Adam said. "I got over my loneliness last night and walking the wall by myself today made me feel at home here. Besides, I'd like to do some writing."

"What about?" Annika asked.

"I don't know. Maybe about my adventures today along the wall. Maybe about you two. Maybe about the three of us."

"Fiction or nonfiction?"

"I think non," Adam replied. "Someone out West, after Zoe left, said to me the problem with fiction is that it has to be believable or at least probable. Real life—what we're doing here, we three—is quite improbable. Just pick up the newspapers any day. No one would dare write fiction about those things. They're too hard to believe."

Just then a loud siren sounded, and Adam followed the two women as they rushed to the front windows and opened them. The siren, accompanied by flashing lights, was emanating from the top of the wall. Twin searchlights illuminated the death strip. A young man, who had apparently been sprinting across it, was suddenly caught in their glare. Two rifles barked and the young man fell. He lay there, twisting in agony, bleeding out into the sand.

Zoe and Annika shouted at the guards, joining the cacophony of sound emanating from all the apartment houses facing this section of the wall, but the guards who had shot the young man made no move to get him to a hospital. The pool of blood expanded. After a while, the young man stopped moving. It was clear that he was dead. A truck, not an ambulance, drifted towards the spot where the young man lay. Workmen picked up his body, tossed it into the back of the truck as if it had no more importance than a sack of beans, and drove off. A guard came down from the tower and began to rake the sand to cover the blood. Zoe and Annika were crying. Adam put his arms around them and pulled them close.

Later he asked the women if they still wished to carry on with the evening's regular activity.

Annika, her face wet with tears, said, "That dead young man makes it even more important that we go on."

"Okay," said Adam. "Let's dedicate tonight's reproductive efforts to him."

Zoe got out a bottle of wine and poured three glasses. They drank a toast to the young man.

That evening Adam had no problem ejaculating into the teacup. Perhaps it was the dead young man who gave what he was doing some urgency. He also didn't fantasize about Zoe or Annika but, instead, about Clare—and it helped. He was becoming more and more eager to see her. He kept thinking about putting his arm around her, stroking her hair. The thought of stroking her hair was enough to give him an erection.

Fantasizing about Clare to produce sperm for Zoe and Annika helped on subsequent nights as well. It did seem a bit indecent. He wondered what Clare would think when he met her and told her the whole improbable story, from meeting Zoe at the Grand Canyon to doing his best to impregnate her and Annika in West Berlin.

He debated with himself whether to tell her that he had fantasized about her while producing semen for the two women. Maybe I'd better leave out that part, he thought. Too risky. But perhaps she would be flattered rather than offended. And if he was going to tell her everything…

On his last evening Zoe and Annika threw a party in his honor, inviting some friends for dinner. There were two obviously gay couples, two men and two women, the painter, Bob Davis and his wife, and the rabbi who had supervised Zoe and Annika's Jewish education was also there with his wife. The rabbi looked even younger than in the picture Zoe had sent.

Everyone, including Bob Davis now, seemed to know what Adam was doing in Berlin, but he didn't mind. He was proud: The Great Impregnator.

"I think you've done a wonderful thing for Zoe and Annika," the rabbi said.

"I'm beginning to feel that way myself," Adam replied. "At first it was a task; now it's an honor."

"Yes. What greater honor than bringing new life into the world?"

"What about you, rabbi? Adam asked. "What made you come to Berlin?"

"Well, first, I should tell you that I actually have dual citizenship—German and American. The Germans passed a law in 1949 that said anyone whose citizenship was revoked by the Nazis—or their descendants—was automatically eligible for citizenship. My parents were among the few lucky ones who got away from here late in the 1930s. I came because I couldn't think of a place where what I did as a rabbi could be more meaningful."

"Zoe and Annika for example?"

"Yes, they've been my star students. But there are others too. My wife, by the way, is a German Jew. As a child she spent the war years with her family hiding in Cologne in a half bombed out building. They were helped by a family of German neighbors who brought food every night in the dark. They really were Christians, some of the rare ones—not the ones who just talk about it on Sundays—and at considerable risk to themselves. An Anne Frank story with a happy ending.

"We have a little congregation. No synagogue yet; we meet in our apartment. But there are plans.

"Zoe says that, until recently, you hated all Germans," he continued.

"That's true," replied Adam, a bit embarrassed. "I'm still—well, maybe I should say I was—still sorting out Germans and Nazis."

"Understandable. Fathering German children will give you a permanent stake in this place."

"I know," Adam replied. "But I can't quite get Germany in focus. The most evil country in world history has now become one of the best, at least here in West Berlin and, I hear, the rest of West Germany.

"Maybe the best," the rabbi answered.

"But you've got to admit, rabbi: this is strange."

"The French philosopher, Montaigne, believed that we all contain our opposites. For the Germans the opposites may be extreme." Adam was reminded about what he had thought in the airport en route to India about thanatos and eros.

After the party, Adam helped Zoe and Annika clean up. Then the women got out cameras and snapped a dozen pictures of Adam and pictures of Adam with Zoe and pictures of Adam with Annika. Annika went next door and got a neighbor to come over and take pictures of the three of them together. "Once we know we're pregnant, we'll frame and hang some of these pictures," Annika said.

Then it was baby making time. Handing over the teacup, Adam said, "This being my last night I'd like to sleep with you, be close all night. I'm going to miss you terribly when I leave tomorrow."

After both women had inserted his semen, Zoe said, "The man who may have fathered our children is leaving, and we may never see him again." She began to cry. Adam held her, his own eyes more than a little damp, half out of sadness, half out of joy. Then, realizing Annika was crying too, he held her as well. Both women snuggled up against Adam where he lay between them, and they eventually fell asleep as one.

Zoe and Annika saw him off at the airport. They accompanied him to his gate and then, alternately, kissed him on the lips, again with a certain passion. They each told him that they loved him, and he told them that he loved them as well. He did—different from the affection he'd felt for any woman before—but love, nonetheless. It was a gift.

They group hugged for a long time; Adam was reluctant to let go and the two women seemed equally disposed to continue the hug indefinitely even though Adam's flight had been called minutes earlier and most passengers had already boarded. Finally, Annika said, "You'd better go, or they'll leave without you—not that we'd mind."

Adam had his ticket checked and, as he headed down the jetway, turned and blew kisses to the women. He realized he had never had better friends.

CHAPTER 21

The day after Adam returned to America, just as the university was starting up again after spring break, he phoned Clare to arrange a get together. "How about Saturday night?" he said.

She sounded cold. "I'm busy then, Professor Levin."

"Adam," he said. "Remember? Adam. How about Friday?"

"Busy then too."

"You mean you don't want to see me?!"

Silence. Well, at least that was better than a definitive No! "You sound angry with me."

This unleashed a storm. "First you tell me you had something to do in Berlin that was hush-hush. I saw how hush-hush it was—you and that woman in the airport."

"That wasn't what it appeared to be."

"Okay. I'm so naive I can't tell the difference between a passionate kiss and a peck on the cheek. Also, why didn't you phone me at my hotel as you promised, so I could conduct the interviews with the two German women who converted to Judaism. Was that woman at the airport one of them? Were you too busy with her to phone me?"

"Things were too complicated."

"Sure, they were! Look, I'm just a graduate student, but that doesn't mean you have a right to toy with me. Our kiss on the plane meant a lot me—even if it apparently meant nothing to you."

She was jealous. She cared. Adam assured her that he wasn't toying with her; the kiss on the plane—meant a great deal to him as well. "Look," he said, "I told you on the plane that I would explain everything when we got together. Nothing is the way you think it was. You'll know this if you give me a chance to explain."

"Okay," Clare said, "but just one. Better make it good or I will never see you again."

They met for dinner at Old Man O'Brien's restaurant near the university. Adam got there fifteen minutes early. He wanted to pick a table in a quiet corner to insure he was in place to greet Clare when she arrived. He sat facing the restaurant's front door.

Clare entered the restaurant looking stunningly beautiful. It was a warm night for spring, and she was wearing a sleeveless summer dress with his favorite colors, yellow and orange. At the Grand Canyon, Adam had hoped Zoe would be his future. Now he had similar hopes for Clare. She was different than Zoe but equally attractive—right now, even more so. He felt incredibly drawn to her.

Adam pulled a chair out for her. She seemed taken with his manners but sat down warily, almost trembling. "Let's get some wine," Adam said. "White or red?"

"Both," she said with the hint of a smile. So, there was a chance. Her personality seemed to be sweet like Zoe, quick like Annika, but she was also uniquely herself. The question was: would she still want him after he told her everything? And he *would* tell her everything, beginning with his marriage, then on to the Grand Canyon with Zoe, and finally to his baby-making activities in Berlin.

When the wine arrived, Adam poured her a glass of white and one for himself. "Do you remember the first words in the Hebrew Bible?" Adam asked.

"In the beginning," Clare said.

"Exactly," Adam said. "I'm going to tell you this story from the beginning and up to this very moment. I'll leave nothing out. Some of it is intimate, sexual. I don't want to ruin our chances—you and me.

"I'm a big girl," Clare said.

"It will take an hour—maybe more. And afterwards you can ask me anything you'd like, and I'll answer truthfully, okay?"

"Yes," she said.

So, he began.

EPILOGUE

A dam's phone was ringing. It was Zoe. "Good news and not so good," she said.

Adam covered the phone with his hand and whispered to Clare, who was sitting on their new couch, "It's Zoe." Clare was now living with him—which had certainly brightened up the Walt Whitman Apartments—though they were looking for a modest home to buy across the river from the university. After their long talk in Old Man O'Brien's, Clare had insisted that he include her on any news from Berlin. "If we're going to make a life together, we share everything from now on, especially about Zoe and Annika."

"The good news," Zoe said, "is that Annika is pregnant."

"That's wonderful," he said. "What's the not so good news?"

"I am not."

Adam was disappointed. He had come to care for Annika too, but there had been that passion with Zoe at the Grand Canyon, so he couldn't help feeling that if only one of them got pregnant it should be Zoe. Annika would have been extra; now she was the main event.

"I'm sorry, Zoe," he said. "Truly."

"Do you think you might…"

"Try again?"

"Yes. If it wasn't convenient for you to come here, I could go there."

This was a situation he and Clare had discussed. She had no problem with his activities in Berlin because they had been arranged before their relationship began in earnest. She was sympathetic to Zoe and Annika, wasn't jealous—well, a little she admitted. "But from now on you're either all mine or it's over between us. No more gallivanting around the world impregnating other women. The only woman you're getting pregnant from now on is me."

"I'm sorry, Zoe," Adam said. "I can't do it. There's a new woman in my life, and we're getting married soon."

"Oh," Zoe said. "And did you tell her everything? The Grand Canyon? Berlin with Annika and me?"

"Everything. All the way back to my wife."

"Then she's the one. I am happy for you."

Adam thanked her and added, "But do keep me posted on Annika and let me know when the baby arrives."

When Adam got off the phone, Clare said, "Annika but not Zoe, right?"

"Right."

"A happy, but not a perfect ending."

"I guess that's life," Adam said.

"I wanted it to be Zoe for your sake," Clare said.

"That's really kind of you," Adam said.

Months later Zoe phoned again. "Annika just gave birth to twins, a boy and a girl. We've named them Hans and Anna."

"That's wonderful," Adam said. "Twins! And I guess I'm the father of two children. I'm just sorry one of them isn't yours."

"I am a little sorry too," Zoe said. "But we have two children and will share them completely, so it isn't crucial whether one of them came from my body. We will both be their mothers. Someday you may want to come here and see them."

"Perhaps so," Adam said.

When Clare came home from the university, he filled her in.

"Let's go," she said.

"Go where?"

"Berlin—next spring break. It's only a couple of months away."

"You're kidding."

"No. I'd like to see what kind of babies you produce. I might want to try you out myself someday. And you must want to see your children."

"I do. But I don't want to do anything that would jeopardize our relationship—make you angry or jealous or unhappy."

"Well," she said, "As I've said before, I'm a big girl. And this isn't pure altruism. I still want to interview Annika and Zoe. Two German women converting to Judaism would make a grand finale to my doctoral dissertation."

"It would be a zinger."

"Even if you had a torrid affair with one of them at the Grand Canyon, now you're just good friends with both of them, and they're lesbians, right?"

"All true. The only one I want to have a torrid affair with is you, the one we're already having."

"So, let's go.

"Okay, let's. Maybe Zoe and Annika can be your friends too."

"Well," Clare said, arching one eyebrow, "let's not get carried away."

ACKNOWLEDGMENTS

No book is written by the writer alone. Ideas come from everyone he's ever talked with, everything he's ever read. In the case of this book, there were people who read the manuscript at various stages and were honest enough—and on occasion tough enough—to tell me the truth, and, when I listened to them, magic sometimes made it onto the page.

Principal among them was my wife and companion in all things, Patricia Ard.

A friend, Jeffrey Stundel, had several key ideas. Three former students, all people of talent, were masterful critics and full of ideas, many of which are expressed in the novel. They are Anna Seip, Andrew Waldron, and Connor Bracken. My debt to these five people is one I cannot begin to repay.

Finally, my thanks to my publishers, Jon and Jody Hansen. In the end it was they who had the idea that made the whole story fall into place.

Michael Aaron Rockland
Morristown, New Jersey
September 1, 2020

ABOUT THE AUTHOR

Michael Aaron Rockland is Professor of American Studies at Rutgers University and the author of fifteen books—fiction, memoir, scholarship and creative nonfiction. Five of his books have received awards. His first book, *Sarmiento's Travels in the United States in 1847* was chosen by *The Washington Post* as one of the fifty best books of the year. His novel, *A Bliss Case,* was a *New York Times* "Notable Book of the Year." A book he co-wrote, *Looking for America on the New Jersey Turnpike*, was chosen by the New Jersey State Library as one of the "Ten Best Books Written on New Jersey." Two other books of his were awarded first prize by the New Jersey Studies Alliance. *Married to Hitler* is his fourth book published by Hansen Publishing Group.

ALSO BY MICHAEL AARON ROCKLAND

Stones

A sneaky and beautiful little masterpiece—sneaky because its disarmingly simple premise of a single day spent visiting graves manages somehow to communicate the endless complexity of one Jewish-American family over the span of nearly a century, and beautiful because Michael Rockland tells his story with a generous, generous heart.

—Tom De Haven, author of *It's Superman*

STONES is a novel simultaneously serious and comic. It takes place in one day as its protagonist, Jack Berke, accompanies his aged mother Rachel to visit the family graves in Brooklyn, Queens, and further out on Long Island. As Jack negotiates the congested expressways from cemetery to cemetery, he contemplates the tombstones, the lives of family members who lie under them, the stones that, according to Jewish custom, he places on those tombstones, and the stone that has for a lifetime resided in his own heart.

Available in paperback (ISBN 978-1-60182-300-7) and eBook (ISBN 978-1-60182-301-0).

An American Diplomat in Franco Spain

What pleasure it gives me to encounter an American, a former diplomat, who understands so well our country, past and present, and who is equally at home in the world and language of Cervantes as that of Shakespeare.

—Jorge Dezcallar, *Ambassador of Spain to the United States*

AN AMERICAN DIPLOMAT IN FRANCO SPAIN is filled with Michael Aaron Rockland's experiences as a cultural attache at the United States embassy in Madrid, Spain in the 1960s. He captures episodes of historical and cultural significance as he goes about doing his country's business. Some of his stories are quite poignant while others are quite amusing. He shares with his readers how he avoided shaking Francisco Franco's hand, how he spent a day with Martin Luther King in Madrid, how his son was selected to be in the movie Dr. Zhivago, how he came to know several Kennedys, including Senator Edward Kennedy, Pat Lawford Kennedy, and Jackie Kennedy, and how the U.S. accidentally dropped four unarmed hydrogen bombs on Spain. Throughout these stories, Rockland explains Spanish culture, past and present.

Available in paperback (ISBN 978-1-60182-304-5) and eBook ISBN (978-1-60182-305-2).

Navy Crazy

The book explores the efforts of the Navy to constantly cover its tracks and to live by the code that there is the right way, the wrong way, and the Navy way. Despite the book's serious concerns, it is also hilariously funny and a super-read.

—Angus Kress Gillespie, *Maritime Historian*

Navy Crazy is a different kind of war story depicting the backwardness of military medicine in the mid-1950s. A memoir of a young medical corpsman learning to survive on a locked psychiatric ward for Navy and Marine mental patients at the hospital on the U.S. Naval Base in Yokosuka, Japan from 1955-57. Rockland captures the ward's atmosphere, its flavor, its culture and its language. A raw personal history not filtered, not for the faint of heart.

Available in paperback (ISBN 978-1-60182-298-7) and eBook ISBN (978-1-60182-299-4).

www.ingramcontent.com/pod-product-compliance
Lightning Source LLC
Chambersburg PA
CBHW051652260626
47170CB00004B/1471